About the Author

Adam Osborne was born and raised in Liverpool, England, going to both council school and a private boarding school in North Wales. Adam went on to study criminology at Liverpool's John Moore's University.

After leaving university, Adam decided to follow his lifelong dream to become a writer.

He worked hard at his craft while working as, a shop assistant, security guard and stock broker.

In the mid-2010s, Adam started both a small theatre company and a film company, before closing them down to focus solely on novel writing.

Adam loves hiking, climbing, kayaking, electric guitar, Liverpool Football Club, (Crystal Palace FC too but… hush.) the New York Jets, ghost stories and motorbikes.

Adam is a student at the Open University and is planning on building his own log cabin.

Steel Mountain

Adam Osborne

Steel Mountain

Vanguard Press

VANGUARD PAPERBACK

© Copyright 2023
Adam Osborne

The right of Adam Osborne to be identified as author of
This work has been asserted by him in accordance with the
Copyright, Designs and Patents Act 1988.

A CIP catalogue record for this title is
Available from the British Library.

ISBN 978 1 80016 485 7

Vanguard Press is an imprint of
Pegasus Elliot Mackenzie Publishers Ltd.
*W*ww.pegasuspublishers.com

First Published in 2023

Vanguard Press
Sheraton House Castle Park
Cambridge England

Printed & Bound in Great Britain

To my mother, brother, and everyone
who took the time to read this book.
I thank you.

'The words; all lives' matter, is a racist dog whistle!
- Idiots on Twitter

'There is a happy land far, far away.'
- Folk saying

Part One

Chapter One

George Rule was walking home along a dusty road in the early evening. Watching as the sun slipped down heading under a far-off mountain of grey mossy rock, he was lost in thought.

Little did he know that he was being watched. The man, the leader known only as Cole, sat and watched the boy with dark brown eyes, that went blank, dead; lost evil eyes.

The others waited, as Cole watched. It was time. His foot shot out, smashing into the gas pedal. The old van shot forward, with a roar and scream of tyres, sending dust flying into the air.

George had his headphones in; he heard nothing until there was nothing he could do. The van shot passed him with screaming brakes. George looked up. Unsure of what was happening, he stopped. As the van's back doors shot open the men, four of them, jumped down.

To George the young men looked less like men and more like monsters: huge powerful chests covered with dark sweaters, jeans and black masks that covered their heads and faces. Only shining dark, diamond eyes in the masks were visible.

George just watched. He didn't scream, he didn't run; he just stood, eyes wide.

A monster in the body of a man rushed at him. A large black leather gloved hand turned into a fist. It was pulled back and slammed into his thirteen-year-old head.

He was lucky he blacked out before he hit the ground.

He was pulled into the van, his hands cuffed, legs taped together, eyes covered with the same tape. One of the men jumped at the boy as he made a vague sound. He pulled his arm back, hand in a strong ball crashing into his head. The pain woke the boy who tried to scream through the tape, as the punches crashed over his shoulders, neck, and head.

The monster went on hitting the boy over and over until small pieces of blood flew over the others, who just sat and watched, as if this was nothing. George stopped making any sounds after a while.

The old van went down the long dusty road, rocking back and forth on its rusted springs, as hits were hammered down.

A black and white police car appeared behind the dark van moving in the mirrors. The driver, Cole, watched, jaw tight as the cop car stayed on his rear wheels. Then he watched wide eyed as the red and blue lights turned on, then the scream of the siren. He moved his hand down lower, to his waistband, where a gun's handle stuck out of his belt.

Cole looked at the mirrors, body moving forward for a better look. Then the black and white police car shot out to the side of the van.

Then the cop car zoomed away from them. Moving back into the lane in front of the van, as the copper drove fast to another crime, not knowing how close he had been to stopping this one.

The cop car vanished from view as the van eased its way down the road. Cole smiled.

The sun went down as the van's beams turned on a side road, long, dark and dusty, leading to the large dark mountains of Kentucky. After forty-five minutes of driving, the van was stopped.

The men stepped out; the boy was thrown over a shoulder. The other men took out gas cans. Opening the cans, they threw the gas over and over the inside of the van. One gas can was full and unused; Cole pushed a dry rag into the can, wetting it. Only the tip of the rag was dry, as he lit the rag, watching the flame crawl towards the heavily soaked part of the rag, then he threw the can.

The can arced through the air, hitting the inside of the van. The men didn't stay to watch; they slipped into the tree line, ghost like, marching towards a mountain, the Steel Mountain.

The van went up in flames. The note was already written for the Rule family, left in a shoebox not far from the smoking van; inside the box were pictures of their young son, beaten and bloody. The family would know that they meant business.

Chapter Two

Hanna stood in the middle of the small old fashion town of Speke, in Queens County Kentucky. Speke was built on the blood of three peoples: one remembered, the black slaves of Kentucky; and the forgotten people, the whites in the coal mines and the Asians on the railways.

Speke was built in 1809, and rebuilt half a dozen times, the last time in 1949. A row of red brick buildings stood looking at each other. A large square garden stood before the only grand building, the white bricked, red topped town hall.

The town was lost in time; the town that seemed more innocent than most in America, but that was only on the surface; if one looked closer something else was there.

A dark shadow hung in the air, as it does in all small towns... the shadow of money and identity.

Hanna liked Speke on its surface, but there was a feeling, bad blood in this town. It was the looks people gave one and other, the way people checked the cash in their pockets before entering shops, there was a feeling here, of being close to an edge.

It was a town where one bad summer, a lack of outsider dollars and pennies, could kill the town.

Hanna moved along, coming to a line of pickup trucks with open gates, filled with colourful flowers, plants and fresh sweet vegetables, pulled from the ground only hours before. Fresh pies, cakes and breads where also in the pickups, made by the wives of the farmers and gardeners. Small handmade signs on white boards were next to the pickups saying prices of the items.

The men black and white, mostly white sat side by side, helping each other out, joking about who made the most. The occasional dirty look at one and other was the only sign of bad blood. These working men didn't care about skin colour; the only colour that mattered was the colour green.

Hanna looked at these men; they were a thousand miles from what she knew.

She was not from this Kentucky. Her father was a businessman and her mother a teacher at Kentucky University. It was she who was the gardener. Roses, only red, never white roses. The roses were not to be touched, but to be shown on the social media for her friends to ooh and ah over.

As Hanna walked past the pickups, she spotted an old fifty-something white man, looking at her closely. She was only fifteen and she didn't want anyone to look at her too closely. She was a stranger here; kids her age were at school, or home.

'Fuck.' She had five thousand dollars in the pink backpack over her shoulders.

She had a man, a real man to find, a white man, a killer. A killer for hire in the twenty-first century. This man was forty years old, a man called William Chambers.

Chambers wasn't forty he was forty-two, but he had the body of a twenty-two-year-old line-backer. But the long deep lines in his face, and dark look to his eyes showed more than his age.

He drove his truck down from his cabin, the bright, burning orange of the truck standing out from the greens, browns, and blacks of the woods, where his large and beautiful cabin stood. These woods were his home.

The tyres of the truck bit into the mud, and the pickup rocketed across the terrain. The pickup shot towards town, coming to a stop at the edge of the road that led to town. The town was, after all, the gateway to America.

America was a place that was once his home and now was the place he didn't understand and thought he never would. He looked to his right and left, seeing the large and empty road, bathed in bright sunlight in the summer heat.

He zoomed the truck towards Speke, towards Hanna, towards fate, and towards the chance for redemption and cold-blooded murder.

Chambers pulled into town, stopping the truck in a space not far from the farmers' trucks. He sat in his truck, letting his engine tick over. He moved in his leather seat, twitching his arm, feeling the Smith and Wesson revolver sitting happily under his armpit. On his left hip was the

Beretta px4 Storm, locked and loaded; he never left his home without them.

Chambers sat watching out of the window of his truck, looking for any sign that there was something wrong, or more likely someone wrong.

After a while he opened the door of his pickup., hopping down to the hot tarmac. Grabbing his baseball cap, he put it on his head, pulling out his silver sunglasses over his eyes. He wore a red check shirt, a tan leather jacket, ink blue jeans and tan cowboy boots.

He closed the truck's door, locking it. Looking around him again, he moved away towards the centre of town, going past the rows of pickups selling flowers and foods. He made eye contact with no one, but he knew eyes were glued on his back as he walked.

He moved about the town seeing the looks of rage on some and the cool smiles of others.

He hated both, but mostly the last.

He bought supplies for the month, dropping them in the pickup, shopping fast, moving fast, but without appearing to hurry.

He was not liked in the town, but hell, it was his town too. He was about to get back into the truck when he stopped. How long had been since he looked around the town?

He had a seen, a sign in a window, he thought. A new shop maybe? He shrugged his shoulders, walking back towards the new shop. He saw it, a new gun and hunting shop; he entered.

The shop was dark apart from two large rays of light coming from the bright summer sun shining in through the windows. Chambers looked at the fishing rods, standing like empty flag poles. He looked at the glass cabinets, showing a collation of pistols, revolvers, rifles and other weapons.

Chambers looked at the weapons. The owner was talking to him without knowing who he was. It was fun, he enjoyed it, being a no one again. It wouldn't last, soon this guy would know who he was, then Chambers would see. He bought one or two items and headed back to his truck.

As he did he saw it, he saw it a mile away: a woman, young, twenty-something. Blue hair, overweight, horn-rimmed glasses. She saw him, and started walking fast towards him, from the other side of the street, something in her hand, a bottle. He knew what was about to happen. Without thinking he pulled open his jacket, his fingers unclicking the holster of his Beretta Storm, fingers ready.

The woman was getting closer, her eyes wide, hate filled, licking her lips. She smiled, thinking that he had not seen her. She was so close to him, and she opened her mouth, about to scream, when with shocking speed Chambers turned on his heels, his shopping bag hitting the ground. Throwing an arm up, he crashed his open hand into her chest, knocking her backwards. She tripped over the edge of the sidewalk, falling, doubling up in pain, as the air crashed out from her lungs. She doubled up, dropping the bottle on her feet. Dark red cows' blood splashed over her shoes and lower legs. Her large frame hit the sidewalk; she was on the floor.

Where she belongs, thought Chambers, *in the gutter.*

With his other hand he pulled out the Storm, aiming it at her. She was about to move at him, her face bright red with shock and rage. She saw the gun in his hand and looked up at it, wide eyed. The anger had gone; fear was there now. She rolled to her back, moving away, her eyes locked on him, as he held the gun on her.

She started crying out, childlike. 'He attacked me, he attacked me!' she called out like the coward she was.

Chambers looked away towards the small ring of people who had formed around them. He watched, seeing if any of them where dumb enough to attack.

A girl ran to the crazy blue haired woman on the ground, helping her to her feet. Chambers felt eyes of rage burning on him, as he stood his ground, gun in hand.

A cop came over, and at once the blue haired woman, who wanted the police defunded, started to scream at him to protect her, fake tears falling from her face.

Chambers slipped the gun back into the holster. He looked at the blood-soaked ground, his eyes covered with dark glasses.

He moved away, heading back to his pickup. The people moved away from him, he was lost in the streets before the cop even started looking for him.

The more he lived here the more he wanted to go somewhere else, but he had no idea where to go, or where he would be accepted… if anywhere.

The streets where quiet as he walked, his eyes moving under the sunglasses, looking for another attack.

He made it to the pickup when a voice, young, called out. He stopped, his back to her. His hand moved down pushing his jacket back ready to pull his gun.

When the voice spoke his name again, he turned around slowly to face the person and was shocked at what he saw.

A girl, *Under eighteen, likely under sixteen,* thought Chambers. He saw a black girl, dark eyes, brown hair lighter than her skin, wearing sky blue jeans, pink jacket, yellow top underneath.

Chambers stood back and without thinking his hand closed his jacket over, looking at her, wondering what she wanted. She didn't look like the normal BLM or SJW. She was black.

'You talking to me?'

'Are you Mr Chambers?'

Chambers looked in shock, shocked at being called Mr.

'What do you want, girl?'

'I need your help.'

'Why?' said Chambers.

'It's my brother.' Her eyes burnt at him, but not with hate.

Chambers looked at her, not knowing what to say. But he knew the type, he thought, she was one of them. Time to go. He moved to the pickup, opening the door. When the girl came to him, running fast, she pulled at his jacket gently. Chambers pushed her hand away. He turned, his face growing red; he was tired.

'What, girl!'

Hanna backed away, looking at Chambers, not knowing what to say or do. She needed him to help her, he was the only hope she could think of. And the hope was going.

He had the door open easing into the seat of the pickup, the door of the pickup was closing, it was closed. He was closed to her.

Her mind moved, trying to get him to stop. The engine was running; he was about to slip the truck into gear.

She pulled the rucksack of her back. Pulling the zipper open, she ripped out the five thousand dollars from her bag, and she slammed the bundle of cash on the glass, her face sad, hurt and pained.

Chambers looked at the cash in her hand, then at the pain in her eyes. He dropped the truck into park, looking at her in shock. He sat for what seemed a long time, looking at the cash in her hand, watching the tears rolling down Hanna's face. He slid the window down, his eyes looking from her to the cash and to her. Not knowing what was going on, he flicked the door locks off.

'Please,' she said.

'Get in the truck,' he whispered.

Hanna grabbed her pack, pushing the cash back in. He drove, heading out of town, to a diner; they drove in silence.

Slipping into a parking spot, the two left the truck, sliding ghost like into the diner, heading for a booth in the back. Chambers order a beer, she a diet coke.

The waitress went, and Chambers dropped his sunglasses on the table between them. They clicked and spun on the coffee-ringed, dirty table, then he looked at her. She looked away, looking close to terrified.

'What do you want, girl?'

She said nothing.

'I said,' said Chambers, 'what do you want.' His voice was a mean whisper.

'I'm sorry, it's just—'

'Something about your brother.' Chambers cut to the quick.

'Yes…' said Hanna.

'Start at the beginning, talk, just talk.' Chambers was soothing, when he needed to be.

Hanna looked down at her feet, moving the backpack under the table between them. She looked at the man, middle height, large powerful forearms, biceps, wide shoulders and a deep large chest. His eyes where brown but had none of the warmth of hers; they were dark and almost empty. His hair was light brown, nearly blond. His skin, though pale, was tough and rough, weather beaten he lived in the outdoor world, in the cold winter nights, skin exposed in the hot summer heat.

She looked at him knowing he was a murderer; He had killed people and she was alone with him now.

Hanna looked around the diner seeing how empty it was; her eyes turned back to Chambers who was not looking happy.

She looked down at her soda, moving the ice with a straw.

'Talk!' barked Chambers.

Hanna spoke fast, head down, eyes away from Chambers.

'My brother was taken by the Klan.'

She had Chambers interested, his eyebrows knotted in thought. He looked into her eyes, easing back into his seat, never moving his eyes from hers.

'Keep going.' He didn't whisper it, he ordered it.

'He was coming home from a party. They took him, he was grabbed. A note was sent to us… his family.' She added the words "his family" fast, as if she needed him to know her family.

'How much?' hissed Chambers.

Hanna looked down, uneasy. It was hard for her to talk about this, especially to him as even now she didn't know if she could or should trust him. But she knew she had to make a decision about him. She looked at his face, tanned, lined, a hard face, an iron face. She waited as long as she thought was safe to do so.

'Two hundred thousand dollars.'

'Does your family have that money?'

She nodded, looking down again.

Chambers let that sink in. It didn't seem right to him. Why would the KKK ransom a family?

Wouldn't they kill the kid? Ransom the government instead? Things didn't seem right. But then maybe the KKK just wanted the money from rich blacks. Whatever the case, if this tale was true, it was bad news for the boy.

'Tell me more,' said Chambers.

Hanna had made her mind up; she had done her research and he was the best bounty hunter in the state. If she wanted her brother back he was her only chance; her mother and father had made too much noise in the defund the police movement. They had been a major part of that, and it had worked a little too well; the police didn't have the budget to do a case like this.

Chambers was a tracker, a hunter, an ex-cop, and he had murdered a black man in New York.

She told him everything, the telling of it was done so fast. The case was clear.

Her brother had been coming home after a party. He left early — no one was sure why — and as he walked home men in a van grabbed him, beat him. The criminals burnt the van down in some wood. His shoe was found by the van and... pictures of him felt. they beat him. The van was left on a country line leading towards Steel Mountain, on a dirt track. A note with the ransom dammed, was nailed to a tree close to the smoking van's bones.

She said all of that, fast, and Chambers had listened, head in hand. He had questions and he asked the most important one first.

'How much for me?' said Chambers.

'The five grand is yours if you take the job. I have twenty thousand for you if you go now, and if you bring my brother back you can have another twenty-five. All in all fifty thousand dollars.'

'Why don't your parents tell me this?' said Chambers, unsure of all this.

'They don't know what to do. They helped too much with the defund the police, the state lost millions to them.

The police hate them, the police lost so much, pensions and work. They won't help us, they can't help.'

'Whose fault is that?' Chambers said with a hidden laugh.

She looked at him, her eyes burning at the insult. 'I need your help.'

'How old are you again?'

'Fifteen.' She had thought about lying, saying she was eighteen, but looking at Chambers, she knew he was not a man to lie too.

'How do you have twenty thousand dollars and another twenty-five?'

'Where do you think?'

She looked over her shoulder, which made Chambers feel very uncomfortable; she was acting like she was in a spy film. And he looked like he was buying her ass. He felt dirty at the thought, they both must have looked creepy.

She put her head down, whispering her next words to him. 'I stole it from my mom and dad.'

'You are paying me with stolen money! how the hell can spend it? Secondly I'm guessing that money is in an account, an account that's not yours. And can be traced to mine.'

'Right, but my mom and dad are progressive. They taught me too much, I have access to their account you must have a...'

Hanna stopped in mid-sentence. Again she looked over her shoulder. It was hard for Chambers not to shout at her to stop doing that.

She continued. 'You must have an illegal under the books account, right. So trace will fail?'

Chambers looked at her, nodding once.

'Good, I can and will put twenty-thousand dollars in it right this second, if you take the job. The other twenty-five thousand is paid when you bring him back. The five you can have now as well if you take the job.'

'You know he's probably dead, right.' Chambers spoke coldly.

Tears formed in her eyes; she turned head, her looking away. She closed her eyes as she nodded. 'If he's… dead, then we bring him back.'

'And I'll keep the cash.'

'Yes, but only the twenty-five thousand.'

He thought long, drinking deep from his beer. He looked back at her.

'No, all.'

She nodded. What choice or hope did she have?

Chambers spoke fast and low. 'But if any cop asks about this, it didn't happen, none of it… understand?'

'Yes. I understand,' she said slowly, carefully.

She went into her bag under the table, taking out a bright pink tablet, and pushing the buttons on the screen, working the tablet in a way that he knew he never could. She turned the screen towards him, showing him a grey page, with the number "20,000" at the top. Under the number was a blank block, ready for his account numbers.

He looked at her, then the number block. His mind raced with thoughts, was this a new set up? But the five thousand in cash, that was an expensive joke, he thought.

'The five thousand too?' Chambers said.

She looked at him once then went down under the table pulling the envelope with the cash out. She pressed it on his thigh; his hand went down, taking the cash, slipping it into his pocket. He needed more information.

'Do you have proof? I need facts.'

She looked hard at him, then pressed something on the tablet and the image dropped away. A news headline came up, with a long article below it. He saw a picture of a burnt-out van, only its bones left in the picture.

He took the tablet from her; if it was fake it was the best he had seen. He moved the image down with his thumb, reading the article. Words popped out at him: kidnapped, Steel Mountain, the Rule family, Hanna Rule, sister of the kidnapped victim.

He looked up at her, thinking hard, then he spoke. 'Okay, let's do it,' he said.

Hanna smiled with relief, pressing buttons. She handed back the tablet. He filled in the blocks asking for his account numbers and handed it back to her.

Hanna went to town on the tablet, pressing this and that. She watched the small round circle spinning around and around in the window. Then the money went into his account, and she showed Chambers; he looked at what it confirmed. She pressed the logout button on the screen.

Chambers took out his phone, calling the bank. He listened to the machine voice. A fresh twenty thousand dollars was in his account.

He turned off the phone putting it back into his jeans, looking again at Hanna.

'I'm guessing you're dumb enough to want come along with me.'

'Oh, I'm going with you.'

'You know that's beyond stupid, right?'

'I'm going, it's my family's money.'

'It's also your life, kid, do you think this is going to be easy or nice? If it's the Klan, they will try and kill us both. They will have their fun with you before they kill you, this not going to be good. Steel Mountain is loved by criminals. Police don't go there, unless they have no choice, even before you defund them.'

Chambers leant forward towards her at these last words.

Hanna knew he was right; her phone was as smart as he was.

Steel Mountain was a bad place; it had been since the civil war and before. The place was filled with criminals on the run, and the KKK had been there too. It was a bad place, she knew that. She had a very good idea what they would do to her, but at the same time, that was her brother out their lost with these racists and here she was hiring a racist to find him.

What was to stop him from just looking in the woods for a few hours, then running off with her money? She had given him twenty-five thousand already, hell, she couldn't let him go on his own, he was a racist. He had murdered a black man and got nothing more than a slap on the wrist. Mostly likely he knew those bastards. Hell, he could be Klan. That was brought up at his trial, the press all had said so.

He could be Klan; he could be in with those bastards that took her brother? What was she too do? Her options were not good.

The cops were all racist, she had been told that since the cot. All cops where racist, as were all white people. And yet where was she to go?

Her family couldn't do it. Her father and mother had never held a gun in their hands in their whole lives. What choice did she have?

'I know I shouldn't go, but I am going!' She didn't look down or away, but she didn't meet his eyes, she looked dead ahead.

Chambers paused looking hard at her, his eyes burning into her, then he said, 'Okay, kid'. And that was it.

Hanna looked shocked at this. Chambers looked at her surprise.

He was taking her; he knew it was dumb to fight with her. He knew if he did she would dig in her heels in on this and would end up being more of a pain in the ass and after all, all he had to do was say he would take her, and hell if she did go into the wilds he'd give her twelve hours, twenty-four at the most, before she would be screaming to go back.

If the boy was on Steel Mountain they had to see one man: Brigance.

'Understand this, kid,' Chambers began. 'If you're still alive when we find your brother, they're not just going to hand him over. There will be a fight. A bad one... people will die.' He said it so flatly, death was just a part of his job. 'If I tell you to run,' Chambers continued, 'just run. I tell you to stay down, stay down. If I say grab a gun and shoot back, you do it. Understand this too. If you die on that mountain I'll leave you there. I can't come back into town with a dead body. That's the rules.'

'Okay,' she whispered, not knowing what else to whisper.

'You have a place in town?' Chambers asked her.

'No.'

'You can stay in my cabin for the night. We go to Steel Mountain tomorrow.'

Chambers looked up, seeing the waitress watching them a little too closely.

'Come on, time to go,' he said, putting his sunglass over his eyes.

Chambers dropped cash on the table.

Hanna grabbed her things, walking fast towards the door.

Chambers walked behind her, feeling the eyes of the waitress on him; he pulled his cap lower, not meeting her eyes but not looking away. She did; her eyes shot down to the counter, counting her loose tips.

They made it to the truck and he fired it up. They flew away from the diner, within seconds it was a dot in the mirrors.

Chambers pulled the truck over, on the edge of a large and deep forest. He moved over to her. Hanna pushed herself back in her seat apprehensively.

'I need your phone and tablet,' Chambers said in a flat, dead voice.

'Wh... why?'

'Because they can track you. I'm guessing your parents haven't given your permission to be here?'

'Oh,' said Hanna.

She handed over her phone and tablet.

Chambers hopped down from the truck, placing them in a shopping bag, which he slammed down hard on to the floor with powerful blows. He tossed the bag into woods, as long and far as his powerful arm could. The bag vanished, crashing into the bush out of sight.

Hanna watched, wide eyed. Chambers re-entered his truck, putting it into drive and shooting away, as Hanna sat watching him.

'Why the hell did you do that?' she said, unhappy.

'The police can track it,' said Chambers in his flat and unemotional voice. He continued, 'If we're doing this, then we don't need the law after us. We're on the wrong side of it now, just as much the people who took your brother.'

'I'm nothing like them.'

'You are now. One more thing, you ever fired a gun?'

Hanna looked in shock at these words, he was already showing his racist side.

'What are you saying, because I'm black that means I know how to fire a gun? You racist pig!' spat out Hanna, her rage up. This was starting to become too much.

'I'll take that as a no, and in future just answer yes and no questions with a yes or no.' Chambers smiled.

'No, I've never fired a gun,' she said in a bratty voice.

'Well, we have to work on that.'

After that they didn't speak, not one word.

Hanna eased back in her seat, looking out of the window, seeing the large looming mountain that seemed so close yet so far away. And on that mountain somewhere was her brother.

Chapter Three

The cabin was large yet rustic. A hand-built house constructed from the trees close by, it was a labour of love, and well done.

The person who did it was a good carpenter, they knew what they were doing. The roof was straight and never leaked. The cabin had been artfully crafted, as had the inside; it was far from the hillbilly one room hut, but more a villa in the woods.

The walls were covered with art; there was even a chimney, made of large grey rocks. A large, wide porch sat at the front. The cabin was two stories and completely open plan, both ground floor and top floor, which was cut in half. The top floor made two rooms, a master bedroom and a guest room. Both bedrooms with bathrooms. The guest room was still, dusty and lonely.

The truck pulled up outside. Chambers climbed out wordlessly as Hanna sat watching him. After a while she opened the truck's door, stepping down into the grass.

She looked around. She had never been to a rural place like this. The trees were so close to the house that they cast long shadows over it.

The smells too were so strong; the scent of the trees, the grass and the wildflowers were almost over powering.

This was a wild place, so different to her world of nice streets, of brick houses, where plants where controlled, never wild.

Chambers went into the cabin. As Hanna waited outside, her eyes glued on the house, she looked at the beams of the porch. They were crafted with ivy vines and grapes going up them. She had never seen that before.

Her house was a good but simple generic building of brick and wood. It was the same as all the houses on her street and indeed the block. This house was different, almost alien to her.

She looked up, seeing a mountain close by. It was large and dark, coloured in greys, blacks, browns and greens. The thing was huge in height. Soon she would be climbing a mountain like that, but that mountain was much bigger than the one she was looking at. She didn't know if she could do it. She was scared to do it. To walk up a place like that next to a killer and a racist…

She knew her country was racist, over ninety percent of Americans were racist. All white people were racist, that was clear to her; look at history. The whites started the slave trade going to Africa, kidnapping her people. Then the Nazis! All white. All evil! A coincidence? Only a racist would think so.

But yet her brother was up there on that mountain alone. Lost. Taken by the KKK, who were demanding money. She had no way to know if he was alive. She needed Chambers, but she did not trust him, and she never would.

She entered the cabin; the inside was a shock. The house was large, warm and nice. It was clearly lived in.

This house was an island, no other word came to Hanna's mind. It was a safe place, a place where Chambers could hide away from the outside world, a place to hide from the people who hated him.

The cabin's walls were made of large thick wooden panels, highly polished and shining dark red. The walls too were covered with artwork; a mix of classical art, folk art, a lot of Native American art covered the walls, as did a large number of classic western pictures, cowboys on horseback looked out from behind glass.

The room had a lot of chairs, but no sofas, just large leather wing-backed chairs covered with throws, white and black ones, mostly sheep and wolf skins. A large white one was on the floor stretching out across the cabin.

On the wall there was a large flat TV screen, looking more like a mirror, then a TV. Around the room was a lot of homemade furniture, a coffee table and dining room table, all handmade.

The living room turned into a dining room, living room and kitchen all in one great barn like room.

The kitchen was also rustic, yct it seemed to be the place where he was the most. A large red 1950s' style fridge was in the corner. There were two ovens, one gas powered one wood powered.

Hanna looked around the cabin, shocked that a cabin could be like this.

Chambers stood in the kitchen not looking at her. His jacket was off, dropped on a chair. She turned to look at him, as he slipped the gun off his belt, dropping it into a kitchen drawer and closing it. It was one of many places where guns and other weapons were hidden.

'Take a seat, relax,' Chambers said, pointing to a chair.

Hanna nodded, sitting, she did what was told. She was worried. She didn't know what or how to feel. Her emotions where spinning, turning, crashing in her mind. She sat very still.

Chambers watched her. He didn't like her being here, but she was. He wondered again if this was a set up and there was still a chance of that. A good chance too that she was lying to him. But a look on the internet had told him that if it was a lie then it was one of the best lies he had ever seen.

He looked at her, seeing her in his home, not knowing what to do and how to feel.

If it was true that the Klan had taken her brother? There had been little Klan action in the state of late. He didn't like it; things seemed odd to him. He walked towards her.

She didn't like the look on his face. Her body tightened. He stopped in front of her, looking down at the young girl.

'What size pants do you wear? Top too.'

She looked at him alarmed. What was he talking about? Was he going to touch her? Rape her?

White men invented rape; she knew that. Her teachers had told her, it was on Twitter. It was a known fact. Would he do that to her? She looked up with deep, fearful eyes when Chambers spoke again.

'I need to know, it's not a perv thing. I'm guessing you don't have any waterproofs. Or hiking boots, any warm clothes with you?'

Hanna locked eyes on him. After a second she spoke and he wrote it down. He looked down at the girl again; his mind made up, he spoke fast. Yet she caught every word.

'Okay, I'm going out to get you some clothes for the hike, I'll get food too. It'll be travel food, the best I can get. But heads up, it's travel food. We eat big tonight; I mean big. It'll keep us warm for tomorrow. Which mountain was the van found next to?' said Chambers. He already knew, but he was hoping to catch her out in a lie.

She answered truthfully. 'Steel Mountain,' she whispered.

'You sure?'

'Yes,' she said in a whisper.

He looked up, lost in thought.

'Is that bad?'

'Yes, very bad. It's a hard mountain. It's a good place for criminals. I almost died on that mountain.'

With that he moved away from her, taking his jacket off the chair and slipping it on. He pocketed her note with her sizes. Pulling the collar up, he jammed a baseball cap on his head, looking at her.

'Help yourself to food and drink, watch TV look around. Please don't break anything or write Black Lives Matter all over my walls. And one thing. No phone calls. No contact with anyone and if you do I'll know and then I'll keep your money, throw you out and let your bother die. Okay?'

Hanna nodded, still not looking at him.

Chambers slipped out of the door heading for his truck. It fired to life and roared away, leaving her alone in the large wooden house. She stood there feeling small. She looked around the house. It was just a house, but she felt odd, strange. She was a stranger in a strange land.

She moved over to the fridge, drawn to it for some unknown reason. She opened the door, looking inside; it was normal. Cans of soda, small brown paper packages of meat, red and white, stacked neatly in the fridge. Home grown vegetables, fresh, in the bottom of the ice box. There was no beer though.

He looked the type to only drink beer but not a drop, only soda. She closed the door and opened the cabinets in the kitchen: normal plates, canned food — a lot of that — all neat, all clean. Spotless, in fact, for such a place as this right in the heart of a wood under the shadow of a mountain. But it was clean, so clean she looked down at the wooden panels of the floor seeing no dirt. High glossy wood shone back at her.

She moved around the house finding that the house of a bounty hunter looked… normal, shockingly so. It was a nice cabin. Which was odd. She moved around, picking up this and that. Was this the house of a bounty hunter?

The only thing that seen odd to her was the lack of pictures. The walls were covered with art and photos, but there were no family pictures, no school pictures, no mom or dad, or brother or sister, a wife or girlfriend, not even a holiday selfie. No nothing.

As she moved around the house, she saw something: a large red metal locker standing in the corner of the room. She moved to it, and though the two small grey vents at the top of locker, she looked in, seeing a line of shotguns and rifles.

She took a step back, a stab of fear hitting her, as if the weapons would come alive and get her.

She moved forward again, getting closer to the metal cabinet, wanting to open it. The doors had a large thick numbered padlock on the locker. She pulled at the padlock; it held fast. Hanna then looked inside again, seeing the row of dark coloured weapons. She looked at them; she had never been around guns, that was something that her parents had drilled into her. Guns were for adults and adults only. She had never wanted anything to do with them. But now after her brother had been taken she wanted them.

It was a secret that was burning inside her, she did want to fire a gun. She wanted to find those people who killed her brother. Her throat went dead, her body cold. She fell forward, crashing into the metal locker, her hand to her neck.

'No.' She whispered to the wood cabin. 'He's not dead.'

Chambers didn't want to go back into town, not after what had happened with the girl who threw blood at him. There was a good chance that she and her friends were still there, maybe looking for him, yet he didn't want to go too far from the cabin.

The girl was alone, and they (the blood thrower and her friends) could come to the house. They could hurt Hanna by mistake, and yet he still didn't trust Hanna, even after seeing the newspaper article. Even after the money. It seemed wrong. She could be setting him up. He could go home to find her gone and a group of men waiting for him, or his house burnt to the ground. It was possible.

But he didn't think so. It was the girl, it was her, there was something in her, her eyes. He had seen that fear in the eyes of dozens of men and women and even children. But this was different, it was fear for someone else.

He pushed the truck fast down the road, as there were signs of the sun slipping down under the mountains close by.

He looked down, seeing his speed: seventy-five miles per hour. He eased his foot from the gas paddle; the last thing he needed now was to be pulled over by the cops. If he got arrested then that girl would be on her own for at least twenty-four hours. She didn't need that and neither did he.

He slowed the truck down, watching the needle ease down as the truck started to lose speed.

He needed to get a grip of himself. He was not in a good place. He didn't like this, it was all way too fast for him. He liked to take his time, to really understand the facts of the case. He didn't have time here; he had the money.

He wasn't ready to go into those hills but within twelve hours he would be in them. He didn't like it. Why had the Klan picked them? The Rules?

He pushed on, going past town, heading towards a big Walmart.

Hanna had been in the cabin for up to an hour and was now eating the food that she had brought in her backpack. She was unwilling to eat his food although he had told her too. But she was worried too, as she didn't really understand him.

Hell, he was a killer and a bounty hunter. What was to stop him taking her money and leaving her up on that mountain? Had she made a mistake to go up there? Could she, could she really go up there on that mountain, gun in hand, like in some western? Hunt for her bother? Everyone thought he was dead, lost in the trees of Steel Mountain. Everyone thought it, but never said it.

She could see it, her mother's tears, the way her father moved around the house, the sideways looks from the cops.

Hanna tried to push those thoughts from her mind. She would go crazy if she kept thinking about it.

She moved around his home, going outside looking at his garden, then seeing two large barns a short walk from the house. She went over to them; both were locked, heavy locks on the doors, numbered ones. She looked at the lock and on a whim she pressed the button on one; the lock popped open. She was shocked by this. Wide eyed, looking at the padlock, she gently pulled it off the door, holding it in her hands.

She stepped forward, her fingers wrapping around the door handle, pulling it. The wooden door shot to the side, moving on its rails, and smashed at the end.

She wondered if he had left it unlocked for her to see, and what would she see? She went to her jeans to take her cell. Her fingers found nothing. She remembered he had taken her phone.

There had to be a light somewhere. She moved to the edge of the wall. Feeling around, her fingers moving over the wood walls until she touched a metal plate. She flicked the switch.

A large bank of lights turned on, showing a garage and workshop. It was clear that cars and motorbikes were his hobby.

There were three motorbikes on the far wall: one very large BMW off roader in silver and blue; a smaller Harley in black, a cruiser; and medium sized green and black off roader — this one looked custom made.

Her eyes raked over the bikes. *So this is the modern horse for the bounty hunter*, she thought.

She wondered if they would take one of them. She stood there looking at the bikes, wondering what it would be like to be on the back of these flying across a mountain. How far could they go up a mountain on a bike? What happened if she fell off? Or if he died? What could she do?

She sat on the floor, her head low, deep in thought. Had she made a mistake doing this? Could she make it in the wilds? What about her mom and dad? What would happen to them, could they cope with her being lost too? What happened if she died on that mountain? But how, how could she leave her brother out there on that mountain all alone?

Chambers' truck pulled up outside the Walmart. The carpark was bare, less than fifteen cars were there. Chambers was a man who noticed things like that.

Chambers put his hand to his belt, feeling for the Beretta Storm then he remembered putting it away in the kitchen. It most have slipped his mind.

He sat back in the leather seat; it had been years since he went out without a gun. He had hold of steering wheel, lost in thought.

This was not like him. He was a hunter, a planner! He didn't forget things. Maybe he shouldn't go. Should he give back the money to her? But what about her brother? Could he leave her and him and her family lost, alone, in pain?

He was an ex-cop, an ex-solider. He had taken those jobs to help people, even after all that had happened and all that had been done to him. Could he just leave her and him?

But he was a bounty hunter now. He shouldn't think about anything but money. Society had turned its back on him. Left him lost and alone. Hated and at times hunted. Now he hunted those in society that were lost... like him.

He sat thinking. He'd do it, he had too. He would go into the wilds and look for her brother. He'd take her as far as she could go, or as far as he could. He moved to the glove box and opening it he took out the small 38 Bulldog; he always had a backup plan.

Opening the door, he eased out, putting the gun into his jacket pocket. He'd get her socks, underwear (that felt creepy just thinking that) and other stuff.

He was fast in the Walmart, moving from aisle to aisle, picking up items as he went. He spent a lot of time in the clothing department picking out clothes for her: socks and underpants, pants that could dry fast, a good pair of walking shoes (for Walmart) and other items. He bought dry foods that they could take on the journey.

He filled the cart and moving to the checkout he bought the items fast too, not wanting to leave her at his place longer than he had too.

Quickly he dropped the items in the bed of the truck. He climbed into the driver's side and fired the engine to life. He flew out of the carpark, the orange truck flying down the dark road.

The USA had been colonized for hundreds of years and yet the mountains and the wilds of American still stood high over man, mocking him, no matter how much of the country was built on and re-built on.

The mountains were always there, standing high, looming over the country, rocky, mossy and grassy monsters that towered over everything and everyone.

Steel Mountain was the one the kid was on, biggest and worse. He's out there lost in the bush. He was dead, of that Chambers was sure; this was a body hunt.

Chambers was lost in thought as he drove. As he got closer to his cabin the street lights went out. The only light came from his truck's two long beams cutting through the night.

Chambers pushed his foot down harder on the gas, the truck's engine screamed, jumping forward. His fingers gripped the wheel, the truck screaming down the road, the tyres burning on the road.

Chapter Four

Hanna looked up, fear pouring though her body as the high beams of a car filled the cabin. She moved out of sight, falling low to the ground. She was anxious, who was this?

Chambers never said anyone was coming. No one, after all, knew she was here but him and her. Could he have set her up? There could be men outside ready to burst through the door take her into the woods and… She looked out from behind the chair, wishing she had a gun or some weapon.

The door open, Chambers slipped out of the truck.

He looked around the outside of the cabin, his hand in his pockets. His eyes raked around the house looking for any signs that someone had been there who shouldn't have been.

He walked around the whole house, looking for sign that she had let someone in: open doors, windows ajar. He saw nothing. All was as it should be.

He was at the back door about to open it when he thought better of it. He didn't want to freak out Hanna, so he walked back to the front of the house. He stopped looking at the cabin; it was odd she had put on the light. The cabin shone, looking cosy.

The cabin was normally dark and gloomy, hidden well in the shadows form the wood. But now the cabin seemed like a lighthouse in the woods. A warm glowing place… a home. He moved forward, pushing away such childish thoughts from his mind.

In the cabin he closed the door. He looked around seeing everything as it should be.

Hanna let out a small gasp at the sight of him, Chambers just stood there, his dark eyes locked on hers. She looked down at her feet, glad it was him. He wondered what the hell she was thinking. He walked past her, without a word.

He dropped the bags on the dining table, moving over to the fireplace. He started a fire in few seconds; Hanna watched knowing that was something that she couldn't do. To just to start a fire in a second, to live here in these mountains and woods, were to her the same as living on Mars.

She looked at the fire jumping, growing as he stood over it, one foot on the handmade stone fireplace. She watched the flames bounce.

Chambers picked up a small dry log, dropping it into the flames and within seconds the light grey log was dark, burnt, burning within the flames.

She had never been in a house with a real fire. This was rustic and yet there was an elegant beauty that she had never thought she'd find here in these hills and woods.

She looked out of the window, seeing the darkness moving closer like a black fog. Soon she would be in that darkness, tracking, hunting a greater darkness and if these woods frightened her...

Then she wondered again for the hundredth time how could she cope out there in the darkness of the mountains and trees. There would be no glass. No cover from it. The night, the dark.

She looked up at the wood of the cabin seeing the wooden beams and roof that covered them.

If Hanna was truthful with herself, this was too close to the mountains already, but how could see not go? How could see just stay at her home, without her brother, lost in the woods taken by those monsters? He needed her!

She had to go and get him. She tried to bottle up her fear, as she looked at the windows the dark.

Chambers watched her, seeing the fear in her face and body. Her whole body was tight with fear. He had looked like that when he arrived in the Marines. He hoped for her shake that it would be easier for her then it had been for him.

He moved over to the oven, turning it on placing in a large amount of food inside. The smell of food came to Hanna and she looked over to him. Seeing a large uncooked pizza in his hand, she watched him place it into the oven above the steaks.

Hanna looked at him, his eyes locked on to hers. He was unsure what to say to her. As a bounty hunter his interactions with clients had been very limited. As he looked into her dark eyes he knew he liked it that way. This was different and a difference he didn't like.

'Wait here,' he whispered, walking out of the room and going to his bedroom. He returned with a small metal lockbox. He pushed the top button of the box, popping the lid open. Chambers took out another Beretta Storm but this time a subcompact.

He placed the box on a side table.

He spoke one word to Hanna. 'Come.'

She did. They moved to the back door of the cabin. His hand shot out, flicking on an outdoor switch and a harsh bright white light fired to life, showing a huge old tree with a round wooden target in front of it. She saw it over his shoulder. When he turned his head to her, he spoke again.

'Get the bullets from the box.'

She went to the metal box and found a pack of red bullets. She took them over to him, holding them with thumb and forefinger not wanting to touch them more then she had to, as if the box itself could hurt her.

Chambers watched her. He saw the way she held the box. He knew she shouldn't go, and she knew it as well.

She offered the box to him, wanting him to take it from her. He looked down at her, a small laugh on his lips.

'Hold it,' he whispered.

He pressed the button on the gun. Catching the magazine as it fell into his hand, he looked at it.

He was a fan of the Storm by Beretta, owning two of them. It was a good gun for to her learn on.

She was a from a liberal family and thought that a gun was an evil thing that white people used to control minorities.

'Look kid,' he said, 'a gun is a tool, nothing more. a. A car in the wrong hands is a killer.'

'I don't do guns,' she said, she had wanted to hold a gun to use it, but now it was so close to hands, she didn't know if she could really take it, hold it fire with it. Kill with it.

Her eyes locked on the small black pistol. It seemed so small in his hand.

Chambers brought it towards her.

She backed away her hands instinctively going up as she backed up towards the wall, her heels crashing into the red wood.

Chambers looked at her with surprise. How could she make out there in the wilds if she were too afraid to even touch a gun? If they found the people who took her bother, they were not just going to hand her brother over with a 'sorry'.

There would be a gun fight. A bad one. A violent one. If she couldn't shoot back then, she would be killed, hell she could get him killed.

'Kid,' said Chambers, eyes rolling 'if you can't even hold a gun, then what good are going to be with me? Make no mistake, we will be in a fight. People will die.'

He pushed out the gun towards her open hands, dropping the little gun into them.

Her eyes locked on the black gun. She was unmoving, heart pumping, she didn't know if she could ever use it.

She knew what those things did, it was firearms that kept her people down. The white man had used them for hundreds of years. Then, through fear, her people had taken the gun towards each other. She knew, she had been told it over and over.

'Kid,' he whispered again, 'if you can't do this then go home. There ain't no shame in that. This is war. Make no mistake! I can't find your brother, get him back and look after you all at the same time. Take the gun or I drop you of at the train station. Pick one.'

She looked at it, then her fingers gripped the gun. It felt normal, like nothing more than a piece of plastic. She held it hard in her hand.

He showed her how to hold the gun. How to stand. How to aim. How to load. How to cock the pistol. How the safety worked. Hours dropped off the clock as she learned.

'Aim,' he said.

She looked down the barrel. A small bright yellow dot of glow in the dark paint sat at the end of the barrel making it easier to see in the dark. She did what he had told her to do. She looked at the end of the gun, she aimed and re-aimed.

'When you're ready… fire!'

Her forefinger shot back; the trigger flew backwards. There was a pop, a small flash from the end of the gun. The gun kicked back. She missed the target, hitting the tree, a small amount of dust and bark falling to the ground softly.

'Good, again,' said Chambers.

She aimed and fired, aimed, and fired, aimed, and fired.

'Good, better,' he said.

As the gun emptied, she reloaded it. Cocking the pistol, she aimed, hitting the target; she was doing well. Chambers stepped back, his hand going to the light switch.

'Aim,' he said.

She did.

'Fire when I say.'

She looked, aiming at the target. Then with a large click the white light went out. The darkness seemed to be painted on her eyes, the target was gone, the world was gone... only darkness.

'Fire!' barked out Chambers.

She did and the bullet shot out of the gun. He turned the light on again. She had hit the mark.

'Faster,' Chambers said, flipping the white light on and off, off and on.

She fired the pistol again and again until she felt comfortable with it, in the light and dark.

Then the cold set in fast; they went back into the cabin, closing the door on the night air. The smell of gunpowder came in with them.

They ate the meals that Chambers had bought and cooked, pizzas and steaks mostly. She ate until she couldn't eat any more. She found it hard, her throat was tight and dry.

Chambers looked at the wall clock and seeing the time he turned to Hanna.

'It's late. Go to bed. You need sleep for tomorrow, we go when the sun comes up.' He stood. 'Follow me.'

Standing, she followed Chambers to the upper floor. He opened the door, turning on the light. She saw a tasteful but dark room.

'Sleep,' he said.

Turning away, he stopped at the doorway, taking something form his pocket. It was the subcompact Storm.

54

He took out the magazine, checking it. Empty. Then the pipe, also empty. He replaced the magazine into the gun.

'Kid.' He threw the gun at her and she caught it. 'Keep it close, don't reload it. Just get used to it,' Chambers whispered.

With that he walked out of the room, closing the door behind him.

She stood in the dark room holding the gun close to her chest. It was empty but it felt safe in her hands. She undressed, slipping into the covers of the bed.

She saw the shopping bags he had brought in from the pickup sitting on a chest of drawers. She heard the footfalls from his boots as he walked through the house.

Chambers went through the house, turning off lights, until only a dim light filled the cabin with small amber pools.

He walked straight to the red metal locker and opened it, looking inside at the row of shotguns, rifles and assault rifles.

He took out an AK-47, dark blue iron and walnut wood. He looked it over, taking it over to the table behind him. He placed the gun on it. He moved back to the locker, taking two extra magazines and placing them next to the AK.

Again he went back to the locker. On the top shelf there was a collection of handguns, all on gun racks, their handles pointing towards him.

He looked at the line of handles; he went to the third from the left, a light bone grey handmade handle. He took the gun out, a long steel A 357 magnum. He looked at it, the long eight-inch barrel in his hand. His thumb slid back the hammer, pulling it all the way back. Looking at the dark blue gun, he pulled at the trigger, watching the hammer crash forward hitting an empty chamber with a satisfying sound.

He went to the table placing it next to the AK-47. These where his tools, his friends, his back up.

The job was starting to take shape. He couldn't trust the girl. He couldn't trust anyone.

He looked at the guns in his locker, the two on his desk. *These you can trust*, he thought.

Relooking at the row of handles staring back him. His hand came out, fingers running down the gun handles until his fingers stopped, finding the right gun. What he needed. He pulled out the Beretta Storm. He also took out two extra magazines placing them all on the table. He looked at the three weapons an AK-47, a .357 magnum and a Beretta Storm.

From the locker he brought out a bowie knife, handmade, placing that with the other weapons. He looked at them, then he moved to the locker taking out two things from it: a small but powerful flash light, that he could place on the AK-47, and next he unzipped a small hard case taking out a large and very powerful scope for the AK-47, sliding it onto the top of the gun.

He removed the magazine from the AK, aiming it at the wall. He pulled the trigger, hearing the loud and reassuring click of the rifle. He did the same with the others. The guns they were ready.

He looked down the weapons. Three guns. One knife. A good collection of weapons. He knew he would need them. He knew he would use them. He wished for more. But he knew he couldn't carry more. He needed speed.

He moved the into his bedroom. He packed his things in a backpack. It took him about an hour. Then he went to bed, sleeping deep and fast, his alarm waking him an hour before the sun came up.

Chapter Five

He woke, showered, dressed, and ate, all in darkness before the sun came up. When the first rays of light came through the trees, his eyes went wide.

Chambers marched to Hanna's room. He opened the door and saw her asleep her body wrapped in the folds of the blankets.

He moved over to her, pressing his hand on her shoulder, and she woke with a start, turning in bed to face him.

'It's time,' he said, turning on the bedroom light, leaving the room.

He went out to the garage and looked at the row of bikes, wondering if he should take one.

There was a good chance if he took a bike that he would lose it. These bikes cost money and twenty-five thousand was not that much. Hell, another twenty-five thousand wasn't all that much.

He didn't want to take any of his bikes if he was to lose it. If the kidnappers were where he thought they were, then it would be a nine-day hike or a day or two on the bike.

Time was the enemy on this one. He did care about the kid lost in those woods. And the girl, she would be a pain, lost and scared out there in the woods.

He'd tell her straight if he was to lose the bike, she bought it.

He wheeled the off roader to the back of the pickup. He placed a small ramp onto the bed of the truck then started the bike's engine and drove it up onto the bed of truck. He strapped it down tight.

Hanna was out of the shower, dressed, her bag packed when Chambers returned. He looked her over, then pointed to her bag which she handed over without thinking. It was and would be easier to let him think for her. He checked it before they went.

'Hanna, we'll take the truck up to see a friend of mine. He lives on Steel Mountain. He'll tell us everything we need to know. If the people who took your brother are on that mountain he'll know or know of it.'

'Okay,' said Hanna.

'But after that, we can't take the truck, the lanes are too small and there's way too much land for us cover on foot. We'll take one of my bikes.'

'Okay,' said Hanna. She didn't like the way he was saying this. She had never been on a bike in her life, let alone deep in the woods, in the wilds of the woods.

'If I lose my bike, or it gets taken, then you or your family owes me a bike and if you don't pay. I'll burn your fucking house down… understand?' Chambers said in icy cool voice of honesty.

'Okay,' she whispered, her eyes wide.

'Not joking, I'll burn it down. I like my bikes.'

'Okay.' She breathed out. Money was the last thing on her mind.

Chambers looked out of the window at the sun rising through the trees.

'Eat,' he said, his eyes transfixed on the windows; it was time for them go soon. Chambers had already eaten, but there was food laid out on the dining table for Hanna.

He pushed over a plate of food. Hanna tried to eat, without too much luck.

Chambers handed her zip up bags of food.

'Put these in your bag. You'll want them later. Trust me.'

Chambers looked away from her, looking out at the cold rising sun. The light was going higher, it was…

'Time to go,' whispered Chambers, eyes fixed on the window, watching the cold golden light move across the glass.

Chambers went to his room to collect his bag.

He put the handguns on his body, the AK-47 in his hand, an axe in the other.

The axe went into the truck's bed.

Hanna felt as if she should say something. They were about to go on this crazy journey to save her brother from the Klan. But no words came to her; this was not a film, this was real. Her brother was out there lost in pines. Lost on the mountain of Steel.

The sun was coming up and she looked out across the inky dark sky, wondering where Steel Mountain was.

Christ, she thought. She didn't even know where the fucking mountain was.;

Chambers opened the rear door of his truck, dropping his pack in there. He took hers too, dropping it next to his on the back seat. His AK went into a gun rack on the roof above the rear seats of the truck, locked in tight.

They were ready for action. He looked over to Hanna it was time her to get into the truck.

'Time to go,' said Chambers flatly, as if these was a normal everyday thing, no different than going to the shops.

Hanna didn't look at him, her eyes raking the inky blackness as the sun rose slowly into the sky.

'Where's Steel Mountain?' she said.

Chambers followed her gaze; she was looking at the wrong place. 'Hanna,' he said.

She looked over to him, and he pointed to the right and higher than she was looking.

'It's a bad place. Cops can't get there in force. Can't drive up the roads, they're too bad and walking is out of the question. It's almost impossible for them to land a helicopter there. Bad people have used it for hundreds and hundreds of years. The Native Americans used Steel Mountain when their own were after them. It's bad, bad karma up there. Haunted, cursed place.'

Chambers watched her. She kept looking into the dark of the dawn.

Chambers moved around to the back of the pickup, taking the last items for the trip; Hanna saw him move and without thinking, she moved around the pickup, looking at the last items: a chainsaw, a large belt covered with water bottles and the other thing made her turn away, about to puke.

She couldn't look at that, they didn't need that. She wanted to scream and scream at him. That… thing was not want she needed to see.

Chambers looked down at the folded black thing wrapped in a plastic. He looked away from her, knowing why she hated to see it. But life was life. And facts were facts.

He picked up the thing, moving it to the bike. He undid the hatbox on the bike, then put the thing in the box, placing a bullet box on the body bag.

Hanna stood, her hand over her mouth at the side of the pickup.

She looked at the log cabin, trying to force her mind to think of something else. She liked it, she liked it here on these hills. The cabin was so beautiful, she wished she could stay. She should stay here on the hillside in his cabin and wait for him to come down with her brother. But she knew she couldn't trust his gender, his skin or his culture.

He came around to her about to speak, to say the same thing she was thinking — she should stay! — but before he could open his month, she opened the door fast, entering the truck, slamming the door after her.

Chambers looked at the closed door and going over to the driver's side, he opened it. He sat in the truck, turned the key in the ignition. Waiting, he looked straight ahead, not meeting her eye, as he spoke to her.

'Even now, Hanna,' he said, 'it's not late to turn back.' Chambers said all of this with his eyes locked dead ahead of him.

She moved forward in her seat, looking at the log cabin in the mirror. 'God, I wanted to stay.' She thought she knew she should stay. Ahead of her was a world of cold, pain and monsters in human flesh. Out there on that mountain. 'Just... drive,' she whispered.

Chambers waited for a second then he popped the truck into first gear. Moving his feet in perfect time, the truck went forward fast.

Chambers didn't look back at his home, but he had a feeling that he would never see it again.

The truck flew down towards the long road that led towards Steel Mountain and Hanna's brother.

Part Two

'Hope is a dangerous thing' — Red.

Chapter One

It is cold in the early hours of a July morning in Kentucky. Yet Chambers big orange pickup was warm.

Hanna sat in the passenger seat, head low, the cold outside, the warmth inside, the early start with the promise of long hard days ahead of her. Her head lowered and lowered until it dropped onto her chest and she fell into a deep sleep.

Chambers sat driving the pickup faster and faster. He heard the soft, deep, breathing of someone sleeping. He didn't need to look over at her to know that she was asleep.

He kept his eyes on the black road, flying towards the mountains. Flying towards that one, to Steel Mountain.

It was a monster, a truly dangerous place. Steel Mountain was one of the biggest mountains in the state but also one of the most overlooked mountains in the state. It had a bad reputation; criminals used it, and only criminals, only one good man was on that place.

The mountain was a hard one, made mostly of trees, woods, hard rocks, boulders, fast deep rivers and lakes, and cliff faces. Loose rocks made hiking very tough, as the wet seasons in Kentucky made the rocks almost impossible to walk on. As foot holds are hard to find, every step on the rocks slides you back.

The mountain had almost no useful minerals and no way to get up to them, or to get them down. In the history of the state there was only one mine on Steel Mountain. That lasted only a year.

Even today it was a hard place, heavy trees, thick canopies make landing a chopper almost impossible. Criminals knew this. That mountain was filled with hardened vicious killers and their victims.

Her brother was on that mountain; he had been for about a week. In Chambers' mind he was dead on that mountain… somewhere.

Whoever took him was most likely still up there to. They would stay until the money came through and if they were smart they'd stay on that mountain for a week or two after the cash came through. He wondered who had taken him. The girl thought it was the Klan or some other white power bullshit group.

God I hate them, head thought. The white power groups had made his life unbearable, just as much as the black people who screamed at him that he was a racist.

Christ, he heard that every day of his life for over a decade. Every time he went out of his house he met them shouting, screaming, eyes wide and hate filled and almost all of them where white.

The mountain loomed over them as they drove into its shadow and yet they were still hours from it.

He looked down at the gas; the tank was almost full, only one quarter was gone, but better to have it full. He looked up seeing the red sign of a gas station on the horizon. He moved the truck towards the station, pulling up to a pump.

He looked at Hanna in her seat, her head down resting on her chest; she was fast asleep. He wondered if he should wake her, then thought better of it.

Inside the gas station, paying for the fuel, he also picked up a coffee and a soda. The brim of baseball cap was low, as low as he could have it with bringing unwanted attention to himself.

He stood by the truck, watching Hanna sleep as he pulled the top of the coffee, drinking it down in two long deep gulps, that burnt the roof of his mouth and inside his throat.

Crushing the paper cup, he opened the cool can of soda, drinking deeply, easing the burning.

He looked out across the horizon; it was still early. The sun was up, but it was still cold. It was not even six-thirty. Soon the roads would be filled with traffic, people going to work, the commuters having no idea what was going inside his truck.

Again his eyes moved to the mountain, it was getting closer and closer, glooming large above them, making his truck seem like ant.

He knew that mountain. It was a place he knew well, it was a bad place, a hard place, a wicked place, an evil place.

Without thinking his hand went up to his right shoulder, scratching the old bullet wound there. He had got that on Steel Mountain and that bullet was all he had got there too; it was a bad place, bad people, bad weather, black bears, a lot of them.

He was afraid for the girl. He looked over at her. With her and that mountain, this could be his death. And for what, twenty-five thousand dollars? He valued his life much higher than that. Didn't he?

He should take her back to town, give her the cash, keep some for expenses and tell her to kiss her woke ass.

Then he looked out again at the mountain. This was bad, really bad, he thought. But he also knew that if he didn't go up that mountain, then Hanna would do something foolish like go alone and she would die.

Another reason was a creeping thought that came to his mind, he hoped. He hoped he would find this kid, kill the bad guys. And he would come down from that mountain sweet and clean and the world would forgive him for a mistake that was almost twenty years ago.

Then came the knowledge that the world would never forgive him, it was dumb to even think it. To them he was a racist, a nigger hating freak, who killed blacks for fun. It was not true. It *was* true that he had killed black people.

Four by his last count, but all but one had been *fair* kills, as he thought of it. You had to think like that, or you would go crazy.

He looked over at the kid. Time to go. He opened the door of his truck. He eased it down the road towards Steel Mountain. His truck was a tiny orange dot zooming towards a grey, green giant. He pulled up to it at seven-fifteen a.m.

Chapter Two

Hanna woke in the truck. She looked out of the windows; all seemed the same to her. The woods were deep, the trees moving in close, their branches moving over them, towards them. Long wooden fingers reached out towards the roof of the truck, as the truck shot passed.

This road was less used. Large, deep cuts had been ripped into the ground. She could feel it and see it in the way the truck moved on the road; it was clear that they were moving closer to the mountain, and away from the normal world.

She looked up though the sunroof, seeing it, the mountain, towering over them. The size of it was shocking, like something from a nightmare fairy tale.

The trees grew in strange, odd angles here. The mountain looked more like a forest than anything else. A cold jungle going up towards the sky. She was in its shadow, it loomed over her, she had never felt so small and helpless. Somewhere up there in those trees and rocks was her brother.

Steel Mountain had been known by many, many names over the years. From the time when the USA was still attached to other countries, it had stood there; it had stood fast against ice ages and more, yet it still stood.

When the first people walked out of Africa making their long and slow journey from that place to here. Over the thousands of years, their bodies changed in order to survive in the harsh North American continent.

And Steel Mountain was there standing high. After more time passed away and more trees grew, wild flowers and bears moved to the mountain.

When the first people of the USA lived there, they too grew under the shadows of the Kentucky Mountains. But that one was different, they all knew it.

The people knew not to go there, bad things walked on that mountain, things that shouldn't be, moving in the darkness of the trees. The darkness climbed into the rocks, inside the water of the small brooks that moved across the mountain's face; it slipped into the might trees and even the grass and mud, into the very core of Steel Mountain.

It was a bad place, a bad land, the locals learned fast not go there. Evil in the shape of men walked there, also evil in shapes of others moved around in the dark.

The mountain was dark, grim, black deep shadows ran across it. No matter the time or season, blackness was on that place. The natives knew it too, they had learned fast, they didn't go up there.

No hunting, no fishing. No nothing. That was Steel Mountain.

The only men who went up that mountain were desperate men; men with guns in their hands and a price on their heads went up to that place. Cruel men. Chambers had been up there several times; he liked that mountain secretly.

Chapter Three

The truck rocked, rolling and bouncing down the road. The tarmac was long gone now. The truck was shooting down a dirt track, littered with potholes and fallen branches, the tyres digging in the dirt and rocks. This was nothing to the truck. This truck could and would handle much worse than this.

Inside Chambers sat, his eyes fixed on the road. The world around him slipped away to nothing, he just drove.

The truck was flying down the road. Engine screaming. He made small changes to the wheel, gently moving the wheel in small corrections, missing the large rocks on the path. The truck could take this and more. It was nothing to his skills.

He was an old hand at off-roading. But he also knew the truck was wide; he didn't need the truck's wheel too hit a hole or a ditch at the side of the road. That could spin the truck, maybe even roll it over. His eyes didn't move from the road.

Hanna hated this. She sat unmoving in the passenger seat, her eyes transfixed on the road, body pressed back in her seat, her hands digging into the chair. Her muscles where tight as a spring, as the fear drove deep into her.

They had shot past the main path for the mountain. She had seen the small rusty, weather-beaten sign that named the mountain.

She had thought that was where they would park and go on foot, or motorbike. But no, the truck was flying on, going higher and higher.

Then she thought this was his land, his world; he knew where to go and what to do.

She looked at the grey, green rock high above them. It made her mind race.

She had visions of that thing, that mountain moving, sliding down towards her. Just slipping down, trees, rocks and mud moving in waves at the truck, covering them in wet mud, rocks and trees, drowning them in it, the pickup lost under the mountain, trapped under the mountain, as wet sticky mud came in through the windows, filling the cabin of the truck and filling her eyes and lungs. She shivered at the thought.

Her heart beat faster and faster the closer they moved to the mountain. Somewhere, he was on that mountain.

God, she thought, *I hope he's alive. But how long could he live out here in this terrible place. Fuck.* A week had almost gone.

She had read the statistics online about kidnapped victims. She had a voice in her head getting louder. It said one thing over and over, that he was dead on that mountain. She was going there for his body.

'No,' she almost called out in the truck. 'He is alive,' she whispered angrily.

She was in a fight, she a fourteen-year-old girl in a fight against fully grown men with guns and the skills needed to use them.

She had never fired a gun until a few hours ago, how could she win? And as she looked over at Chambers, he was a good bounty hunter, but he was a racist, he was white after all.

If he was alive, she had to be there. She couldn't trust Chambers.

She looked over her shoulder seeing her backpack sitting on the backseat of the truck. Inside was the gun. Soon it would be in her hand, and she would need it.

With all her heart she hoped that this could be done in a day. She hoped they would find him and find him fast.

Chambers would go in there with the rifle and get him.

She looked at her watch, almost nine a.m; the sun was up and hot, yet she shivered with fear. It was August 19th and she thought on this day or 20th she was most likely going to use that gun in her bag and use it on another human.

The truck started to go; they were climbing the mountain more sharply.

'Oh God,' she whispered to herself. When she came down this mountain she could be a killer.

Her hands moved over her mouth, fingers digging across her face, her hands covering her lower face. Only her eyes looked out, which were wide when she saw it, the path heading higher into the mountain.

It was a grey steep path, a real climb for any car or person and it was going up. To the right was a wide and deep wood.

Chambers pushed hard on the gas pedal and the engine of the truck screamed as the truck shot up the path.

There's no turning back, Hanna thought. She almost screamed, 'I want to go home!'

Chambers sat back in the truck's seat. He had seen the girl moving in her seat. Chambers pushed the truck harder and harder up the path. The mountain, the job. That was what his mind was on.

Chambers knew what she thought of him. He didn't care. He had a double job to do: get the kid out, keep the girl alive. He doubted he could do both, but he was sure the boy was dead.

He pushed the truck up the mountain, no longer in its shadow but a part of it. They moved up it at a fast rate, towards one thing: Brigance, the only good man on that mountain, the gatekeeper to the evil of Steel Mountain.

Chapter Four

Brigance stepped out of his cabin/shop/bar/information centre, pulling out the Beretta 92 from its holster, pulling the hammer back, standing framed in the open doorway, bouncing on his hiking boots. He wore light blue jeans, a brown and Green coat topped with a brown cowboy hat.

His cabin was the last house on Steel Mountain, gateway to the deep dark that stood behind him.

He had heard it, the deep roaring, cutting, scream of a large engine.

He stood listening and watching, eyes raking the treeline. The truck wasn't here yet but the sound was. It was coming and getting closer.

With his dark-skinned thumb, Brigance pushed the hammer backward, cocking the gun. Without looking, Brigance sat down on the handmade bench and waited.

He wondered who it was. It was rare to hear a motor coming this way, very rare. Hell, this was Steel Mountain, no one came up here in a car, only on foot, some of them just about alive.

The truck was bouncing along the small track. Hanna looked ahead, fingers digging into the armrests, marking them with long, thin, white nail scratches.

The truck was so big, too big for this track. The wheels kept dropping down, into potholes and ditches, digging into the mud and grass of the mountain.
The wheels kept hitting rocks, forcing the truck's wheels this way and that. The wheels kept trying and failing to get a grip on the mountain. The mountain itself was a blur as the truck went zooming, making the inside of her belly scream. Chambers was in his element moving the truck faster and faster. The truck was screaming into the woodland, the heavy wheels smashing into the tree branches of woodland floor, as he pushed the truck at speeds that were not safe.

Hanna pushed back deep in the seat. She wanted to scream at him to stop the truck to just stop, to let her out, and to go home. Yet she knew she couldn't. What could she tell her family?

'Yeah I went to the mountain, after spending over twenty-five thousand to save my brother, but I gave up when I got car sick.'

She had to be strong.

Chambers loved this; this was driving. His eyes scanned the woods seeing at shocking speed the right path to take, how much lock to use on the truck steering wheel, how much power to use for the truck, when to move his foot off the gas, and when to let the truck just ease around bends or trees.

Chambers put his foot on the brake gently and the wheels screamed kicking up rocks and other woodland debris, which went flying around the vehicle.

The path seemed gone, just the woods of the mountains.

Maybe it was nature's way of telling them that their world was over. The manmade world was now behind them; they were in nature, the unknown. It was hiding under a mask of familiarity.

The engine roared as if Chambers was answering nature with the defiance of steel.

Chapter Five

Brigance watched and waited for the car. He knew it was something like a car, most likely a truck. He heard the engine screaming across the plains; it was getting closer and closer.

He undid the coat that covered his body, going down just past his waist and popped the holster that was happily sitting on his belt. In the holster sat a powerful Beretta 92. His fingers touched the grip, thumb pulling back the hammer. He waited. This was Steel Mountain and he knew this was no hiker. This was something to watch out for.

Most people who came here, to Steel Mountain where criminals or people hunting them. The hunters where normally as bad their prey. Lucky Americana had defunded its police force. After that the bounty hunter business was booming. People wanted justice and revenge.

Yes, sir, after the 2022 defund the police campaign, bounty hunting went into full swing. The business was booming. If it had not been for the large bullet hole in his upper thigh then Brigance would be back hunting.

Brigance saw the flash of orange and he gently pulled the gun out of its holster, hearing the sound of gun metal on leather. Brigance looked like a man just relaxing on his porch, except for the pistol in his hand.

The flash of orange reappeared, then was lost in the rise and fall of the green plains.

Brigance's eyes narrowed; he knew that sound. He knew that colour. That was the sound of a V8 screaming. He knew who was behind the wheel too. Without thinking, his hand pushed down on the pistol as he replaced the firearm to his hip.

The truck, orange as the fruit, came screaming into view. The large pickup truck was in the air, then smashed down hard on the grass. He could see the man inside was fighting the truck. He eased off the gas, letting the truck just slide.

Brigance stood, his hand on his brown cowboy hat pushing it back.

A wide smile on his dark face, he saw it was Chambers. It had been ages, years since he had seen him.

He hit the wall of his shop in three fast knocks. His wife was sitting at the counter, waiting to see what would happen. She took her hand off the shotgun hidden under the counter, took out the magazine from below and started to read it again.

Chambers moved the truck around in an arc stopping outside the cabin. With a smile and without looking at Hanna, he moved out of the truck, walking towards Brigance. The two met, hugging. They remembered years ago when they meet fighting in the Middle East.

Brigance had taken a bullet for Chambers. Chambers had taken a blade that was meant for Brigance in his side.

The two smiled at one and other and pressed their foreheads together, their eyes burning into one another.

Hanna watched from the truck, shocked. Why would any black person in the world want anything to do with Chambers? He was a racist, a killer. She was using him to find her brother.

She wondered what was next. It was over twenty-four hours since she had run away from her family. She thought of her parents, wondering if they had even noticed that she was gone. They had too, surely, then she thought back to the last few days.

Her family screaming into the phone trying to get the police force to do their job, forgetting that they had campaigned for years to have them defunded.

The police didn't have the money to do anything to help. She thought back to the hours lost watching her father, his head down, thinking, hoping, crying, wondering what to do; her mother walking back and forth or working on social media, starting walks.

They were lost in their worlds of fear, and a lack of understanding of what to do.

She knew in her heart how important it was to them to be seen doing something. Even if it was meaningless. Hell, to be seen doing everything and yet doing nothing was what they did.

Her mind was breaking under the pressure though. She wanted to go from this place, away from this mountain, these woods deep and dark. This place was not right. This mountain was toxic, she could feel it, a deep something, something dark in her mind, that the mountain had brought to life.

She looked over at the two men already moving away towards the cabin.

She hadn't seen the black man, and he was looking at her with surprise. She watched as Brigance and Chambers went into the cabin, as Hanna sat in the truck, not wanting to set foot on that mountain until she had too.

Chambers walked fast behind Brigance and waved once to Brigance's wife.

Brigance led Chambers to the back of the cabin, opening a door to a large wide room. The room was in keeping with the cabin but was much more rustic than Chambers' cabin. It was colder and darker.

Brigance moved to the back of the room, opening a cabinet, taking out a large clean bottle and two fancy glasses. He quickly filled the glasses with the dark brown liquid, moving towards Chambers.

Chambers looked around the dark room. He was a proud, self-taught carpenter, spending many hours on his cabin, making it look perfect.

Here there was only one window in this room and it was facing the wrong way at this angle; there would be next to no day light even in high summer.

He looked at the wall where he could see small pinpricks of light shining though, thousands of them. Bad weather would soon break down the panels of the building, and rats would come though.

Why didn't Brigance let him work on his cabin?

Looking at the walls he saw flags covering them. They had not been there on his last visit. With surprise he turned to them, seeing the flag of the USA but next to it was the red flag with a blue X on it, the sign of the South.

Chambers turned to Brigance as he came to him, a drink in hand.

'Dalmore whiskey, the best,' said Brigance, handing Chambers the glass.

Chambers let out a loud and almost cartoon laugh, taking the glass in hand, muttering in a schoolboy style as he brought the fine whiskey to his face. 'Can I smell it?' Chambers said.

Brigance laughed, feeling like a teen again with a fake I.D. as Chambers brought the drink to his nose, breathing it in deep, then with a great pain he lowered the drink to the table, gently pushing it away. Brigance raised his eyebrows but with little surprise.

'Business,' said Brigance.

Chambers still seemed to be having fun with the smell of the drink. Without opening his eyes he spoke. 'Business.'

Brigance took a sip, unsurprised. 'That's why no drink?'

'Yeah,' Chambers replied, opening his eyes in the dark cabin. 'Quick question?'

Brigance was surprised at the tone; it sounded a little darker than he thought it should.

'What's with the Klan flag?' He pointed as Brigance went to a small cooler, taking out a soda and sliding it towards Chambers who thanked him, popping it open, taking a large mouthful.

'Klan flag!' said Brigance, almost spitting out the words.

'Yeah,' said Chamber a laugh in his throat. 'That's a Klan flag.' Chambers pointed over his shoulder to the red and blue flag that was hanging on the wall.

'That's a classic southern flag, it's the sign of the South,' Brigance said indignantly.

'I thought fucking your sister was the flag of the South?'

Chambers smiled evilly. This was a dance, a game that he had played with Brigance for years, having childlike teenage banter back and forth. Both men liked to push the other to the edge, to the point there you almost throw a punch but all in good fun.

Brigance opened his mouth with fake shock, thinking fast for a good come back. 'From the white man who grow up in Harlem, your fake whitey.'

'I know, you're the black man from the deep south, you're a fake black, black man hoping to be white. And I'm a white boy who should be black, from New York. Anyway I have business.'

Brigance's playful smiled turned to a business smile. He lowered the glass, his eyes dark as they gleamed.

'Who's the girl?' Brigance said.

'Hanna Rule, uptight girl. You know, one of those, everyone's racist but me, and people who think just like me and us alone. Everyone else is racist.'

Brigance let out a bark-like laugh, taking another slip of whiskey.

'So why the hell is she with you, nigger killer?'

Chambers eyes filled with rage, boring into Brigance's. Brigance lowered the glass, knowing he had crossed a line. He didn't look at Chambers, Chambers' chest moving up and down with deep breaths. Brigance was about to speak when Chambers cut across him.

'Forget it.'

Brigance spoke, trying to fix things. 'Chambers.'

'I said forget it.'

'Cool and I'm sorry. Anyway why on Earth is safe place girl with you? And why are you both here? This is Steel Mountain. Only children on this mountain are kids forced up here... you didn't...'

'No, I didn't, believe me. She's crazy as fuck and hate-filled. She's just a parrot, just saying the same stuff her parents have told her. But it's bad.'

His body language changed, becoming stiffer. Brigance noticed it and he looked deeper at Chambers; something was up. He was on a job then, it came to Brigance.

'A bounty?'

'Yeah, her kid brother has been kidnaped. She thinks it's the Klan'

Brigance let out a small laugh. 'People like her think the Klan did everything bad, or just white people.'

'Yep, I've had it for hours. Anyway her dumb ass family made the defund the police happen. Cops don't have the manpower to go after the kidnapers or kidnaper. So she paid me to do it.'

'Yeah the bounty hunting market has gone crazy, you know how many hunters been up here?'

'No.'

'We used to have a one a month, last two months it's been over fifty.'

'And they thought,' Chambers nodded towards the wall, towards Hanna, 'that taking huge sums of money from the police, would make them and the world a better place.'

'Yep and how did that work out?' Brigance said.

'You tell me, pal. This fucking mountain is the Mecca for criminals.'

'I know, it's been mad. Great for business but bad people. These assholes have no idea how to live in the outdoors. If they need food or anything else, it's my place they come to.'

'And that's why I'm here. You sold anything a kidnaper would need? It'll be one man, young, I'm thinking the runt of the litter. He'd be jumpy buying because too much food for one person, at least enough for three or four people.'

'Oh, hello Sherlock, when did you become detective king?' Brigance said in surprise at his friend's breakdown and at how right he was.

'I've been hunting criminals since we came back from the desert, officially and unofficially,' responded Chambers. 'So,' he continued, 'seen anyone like that?'

'As a matter of fact... yes. A kid, eighteen if he was a day. Bought a lot of stuff and at random too. He had no idea what to buy, he just grabbed stuff from the shelves and paid with cash. He had a lot of cash on him too. Then went fast.'

'How much did he buy?'

'A lot, I'd say about five days' worth.'

'Five! You sure?'

'Yep. That's why it stood out in mind. Most people buy enough for one person for twelve hours, a day, maybe two. He bought for five guys too. Five guys easy.'

'Shit,' said Chambers. That was more, way more people than he thought. Good job he had the AK-47.

'How do you know it's him you're looking for? I've had a lot of men coming through here.'

'For sure I don't know it's him, but a van, quite big too, was used in the crime. Seemed unlikely only one person would need it. Kidnapping and ransom are hard. Most criminals won't leave the victim alone, too many things can go wrong. It's not a one-man band.'

Brigance's nodded, made sense. But if he was wrong then he had put all his eggs in one basket. And that kid was dead.

'If you're wrong and word gets to the kidnapers that a bounty hunter is after them, they'll panic and kill the boy.'

Chambers looked at Brigance as he spoke. 'Where did he go, did you see?'

Brigance smiled. 'Of course I did and get this.' He stepped out of the room, moving to the open door. Chambers followed seeing the great plains he had driven up framed in the cabin door.

Within a second Chambers and Brigance stood at the side of the cabin, Chambers next to his friend watching him as he pointed out towards the great forest on the mountain. Chambers followed Brigance's finger, wondering what he was doing. Brigance was not normally this dramatic. Chambers looked, then looked again, shocked.

'No way!'

'Oh yeah,' Brigance said with a smile.

'No fucking way.'

'Yeah,' Brigance said again, with a grimace.

Chambers turned away from the mountain. 'That the miners' path,' he said, more to himself than Brigance.

Brigance turned to face Chambers placing a soft hand on his shoulder all traces of fun gone from him. 'Yeah, he went to the miners' path, no doubt about it and I mean no doubt.'

'That's heavy shit, man, no one goes there. The place is littered with open mine shafts. No one goes there. Fuck, these are heavy fucking guys.'

'Yes, drop the kid. Go halfway there then come back. Say you can't find her brother and go home.'

Without thinking, Chambers' hand went to his belly, his hand moving over and over up and down a small part of his belly. Brigance looked down seeing Chambers' hand moving over the scar of the gunshot wound, a gift from this mountain and that place; the miners' path had almost killed Chambers. A 38 bullet was embedded in his belly.

Brigance remembered that, over two years ago, Chambers pulling himself along on his hands and knees, blood dripping nonstop from the gunshot wound, firing his pistol into the air to get attention.

'I'm going after him, the kid.'

'The girl's brother, why?'

Chambers didn't answer

'How long has he been taken?'

'About a week.'

'A week,' laughed Brigance, without humour. 'He's dead.'

'I want to find him.'

'But he's dead… too bad, so sad. Why do you have to die… for that brat! Who clearly hates your guts?'

Brigance paused, looking from the girl to Chambers, catching her looking at the two of them hard. He looked from her to Chambers then to the mountain; slowly he understood why Chambers was going there.

The miners' path was a place where only the desperate went. It was a bad, hard, rocky place, with open mine pits, and there was something else: the amount of people who had died there was overpowering; you could feel it in the air, in the trees and waters. There was something there on the miners' path… only one word came close, and no one would dare say it… Haunted!

'I'm so sorry,' said Brigance. 'Really I am, you shot that man in good faith and the world fucked you. But these people,' he pointed at Hanna, 'will never forgive you. If save that dead boy they won't forgive you, never as in ever.'

'I know,' said Chambers 'but you never know.'

'What else about this kid who came into your store?' said Chambers, going back to business. This kid could be the key.

'Oh, him, he wasn't white; he was a brother.'

'Not shocked, never thought it was the Klan, they're political and dumb. I need a favour, well two, actually.'

'Okay, what are they?'

'The girl needs to stay, here.'

'That'll be hard.'

'Maybe not. The road up here was hard and you're the gatekeeper for the real mountain. It gets much, much worse when we pass your cabin'

'True, but she won't like it,' said Brigance.

'I think if she does come with me she'll quit fast, and I'll send her back here. But I'll have to take her, and time is the enemy here. I want you to keep her here.'

'I can't hold her here.'

'I know. That's not what I'm saying. Tell her, it's best that she stay here until I come back, with her brother.'

'Okay, I'll try, and the other?'

'My truck, I'm taking the bike up here. It's going be a twelve- or fourteen-hour ride or a two day to two-and-a-half-day hike. I want you to look after my truck for me, please.'

Brigance knew he would. It was a simple request. He looked out at the orange pickup.

'Can I drive it?' he said with a small smile.

'Yep, of course you can, only fair.'

'Deal,' said Brigance.

'As long as you look after it.'

'Of course,' Brigance's said, his eyes locked on it.

'Good I'll be off then,' said Chambers, turning towards his pickup, getting ready to move the bike off the back.

He had gone three or four steps when Brigance's voice, hard and sharp, cut into him. Chambers stood, his back still to Brigance; after a second he turned. Brigance's eyes burnt into Chambers, almost pleading. 'That kid,' said Brigance said with a nod to the trees and hills, 'has gone to the miners' path on Steel Mountain. Only serious motherfuckers go there it's a bad cursed place.'

Brigance feared that this would be the last time he would ever see Chambers, the last of his wartime friends. If he went up there he was a dead man. It was impossible for him to put into words how he felt about his friend, about the shit that he had been through. He couldn't say it, fuck, there was no way to say it.

'Miners' path, Chambers,' was the best he could do.

'No matter what happens, I'll be all right,' he said, nodding once, walking away.

Brigance lowered his head, going into the cabin, hugging his wife, kissing her softly. His wife hugged him back happily; she was pleased he went to her when he was in pain.

Chambers walked fast across the plains and at once Hanna moved to him. Her blood was up. She hated this, to be ignored; she was special, and she was frightened. She stormed at him, her shoulders low, about to scream.

'What did you find out?' Hanna snapped out.

'A lead, something to go on, something good too, I think.'

'*What?*'

'Your brother is most likely at a place I know called the miners' path.'

'Good, are we going?'

'No,' he said softly.

'No!' she said, harshly.

'I'm sorry, kid,' Chambers said in a soft voice.

'I'm not a kid, don't call me that!'

She screamed hysterically. Chambers' patience was thin on the ground; this brat had been pushing him hard. Who the hell did she think she was talking to?

'Look, you're done, brat.' He spat out the words at her.

Hanna paused, taken aback at the sound of his voice cutting though her. But she had known this was coming. He was a racist after all and little he had done had changed her mind. In fact the more she was around him the more she disliked him. She secretly hated the fact that he was out there in the wild, and not her father. She hated that fact that deep down she knew, Chambers was a real man and her father… she needed him, really needed him, he was her protector and she found that secretly sexy. Her blood was up; she jumped towards him.

'I'm not a brat.'

'Yes you are, kid, you were born and raised one. You know nothing of this, of this mountain and the people on it. How are you going to deal with that?' he said, pointing at the hills, rising high into the sky, hell the mountain itself was hard, let alone the things on it.

He pointed out across the woods that lined Steel Mountain and the heavy grey, black rocks that stood high above them.

Hanna stood still. Her youth was clear, her eyes glazed as she stood holding her hands to her chest, muttering too herself. Chambers was mad. He was sick of her, sick of her rudeness and her racism.

She was done and she knew it. She had done good to get this far but it was over. He couldn't look after himself, and her, and get her brother's dead body, off this fucking mountain all at once. He was not superman.

She was arrogant! Did she really think that she could make out there? On Steel Mountain?

Her with her upper-class life of pure privilege, cloaked in her childish millennial ways, being taught over and over she that she was the victim because of the colour of skin and that's all she was.

'I'm done,' snapped Chambers, walking fast away from the girl. She stood looking at his back, unsure of what to do. She did want to go home; she wouldn't go home.

'Go home, kid, it's done. You are done.'

Chambers still had his back to her as he jumped in to the back of the truck, lowering the tailgate of the pickup, kicking down a small and impossibly thin looking ladder, rolling the bike down it easily.

He went forward with the bike, wheeling alongside the truck, keeping his back to Hanna, saying with very inch of him that she was no longer welcome, that she had come to the end of the line. She stood behind him, watching as he worked on the bike, not seeming to be doing anything at all, just waiting for her to go.

Brigance stepped out of the cabin, fixing his hat, watching the scene, feeling the tension that hung in the air like an invisible fog.

Hanna knew she should stay, but her mind was made up; she wouldn't go away. She would never leave her brother alone on this mountain, as in ever. He needed her; her family needed her to find him.

It was there in the air, the fact that everyone thought that her brother was dead. She had seen enough of this place, this woodland mountain; she would not leave her brother here. She would not allow him to rot here in this evil place. But Chambers didn't care, he was sick of her.

She shouldn't be here; they all knew it too. This was Steel Mountain, a place where criminals were on the run form bounty hunters. Who in their right minds thought that was a place for young teenager?

Chambers moved to the pickup taking off his jacket. He took the dark brown canvas motorbike jacket, throwing it over his shoulders, as Hanna muttered over and over about demanding to go with him.

To Chambers it was nothing but background noise, no different to the buzzing of flies. Chambers opened the rear door of the pickup, his fingers moving over the clips of the AK-47, unhooking it form the roof. Hanna's non-stop talking seemed to be going on forever; he acted as if he couldn't hear her.

He checked the two other guns were both locked and ready to go. They were, as was he. Daylight was burning.

The bike was ready, as was he. He had to end it.

He moved around the bike, facing her. Her face was a picture of rage, covering her features, but he was done.

'You're done, kid, it's the end of the line for you stay here. Stay with Brigance I'll get your brother,' he said in a flat empty voice.

She stood her ground, body shaking as rage welled up inside her, hands turning into fists; she was ready to explode.

Brigance moved forward. He could feel her anger, he could most taste it in the air. Something was about to happen between Chambers and Hanna.

Chambers looked at her, seeing her there with her blood up.

'You're done.'

He said it as a fact, not a fight, but simple and plain, his hand, without thinking, dropping to his hip close to his gun.

'Don't talk to me like that!' The words came out fast almost as one word. Her body was shaking, her mind was on fire ready to shout and shriek at this racist, mayonnaise bastard. 'I am *going*.'

'No.' His voice was quiet, yet it rang around them.

'No, if you go without me then I'll—'

'Yeah,' said Chambers, turning his back on her, about to throw his leg over the bike, when a sound came from behind him, a loud sound that he knew only too well.

For a second his leg hung in the air. He lowered it back to his side. Slowly tuning, his eyes met Brigance's.

Brigance's dark eyes where shining with fear; in his hands he held his gun up, outstretched hand, not knowing what to do.

Chambers' eyes rolled form Brigance to Hanna. He saw his subcompact Storm in her hands, his gun. A thin trail of grey, white smoke went up into the air.

Chambers watched her; Hanna looked at the smoking gun in her hands her faced shocked that she had a gun. And that gun was now in her hands, pointing at him. The bullet she had fired had smashed harmlessly down the hill.

'Kid, you're not going to shoot me with my own gun,' said Chambers, his voice of cool, almost unbothered. This was not the first time a gun had been fired at him.

'Fuck you, racist. You are a fucking murderer, and you think I'm letting you get my brother alone! I'd rather see him die!' she screamed.

'Then kill me.'

She pulled back the hammer of the gun. Fighting a river of tears, she pushed the gun forward toward him.

'I mean it.'

'If you fire and kill me then brother will die.' He said, with a simple, cold, logic.

'If I leave him with you and those white supremacists. Then he is as good as dead.'

Chambers moved back toward the motorbike, learning on it.

'Then kill me.'

'I will.'

'So you say,' he said softly, wondering if his forty plus years on this planet would end here on Steel Mountain. That was not a thought that surprised him. But the thought that he would die at the hands of a brat girl with his own gun... that was odd.

'Shoot me,' Chambers whispered.

Brigance watched on. He'd kill the kid if she shot Chambers. He'd kill her!

He had before (killed kids) but that was war. He had his gun out, looking down the barrel, at the back of her head. One quick pull and the girl would be dead.

'Kid, I'm going to make it clear.' He spoke, clearly, yet dead, his voice still and dull. No sign of anything in voice. Not one emotion in his voice. 'I am not taking you any further, you're lucky I let you go this far,' Chambers continued.

His temper was boiling over. This was madness, why the hell was she even here? Why did he take her? It was crazy, this was the real world. Kids did not go on bounty hunts and that was the end of it.

'I have to go. I can't leave him out here alone,' she sobbed. The tears were coming down hard. 'He can't... stay here, he has to come home.'

'I'll bring him home to, you dead or alive.'

'He can't stay here. But you're white and whites are racist, how can I trust you. You're a nigger killer!'

Brigance moved fast and his hand shot out, his finger gripping her wrist, pulling the gun hard and fast. At the same time Chambers moved, throwing himself to the side.

Hanna let out a as her finger pulled on the trigger and a shot flew from the gun, crashing into the grass next to her foot.

Brigance had the girl's hand, holding the gun and her arm low to the ground. Brigance's face was a mask of rage.

Hanna seemed shocked at the idea that a black person would attack another black person, and when one was about to shoot a white one; he must be a race traitor.

Brigance's other hand flew out, snapping the gun from her, then he hit a cruel blow across her face.

She fell down hard on the ground. Brigance moved forward, stamping down hard on her calf and she screamed, her hands cupping her muscle. It was then she knew she was done.

She rolled over, looking through the pain towards the woods and Steel Mountain itself. She knew that Brigance and Chambers were right, she was done. It was over… for her.

Brigance looked at her knowing that she was done. He had seen that look in people so many times that he knew, and she sobbed.

Chambers turned away; he was safe. He busied himself with the bike. It was fine ready to go, despite his fear that it had been tossed around so much in the pickup. He was worried that the bike may have been damaged. He knew it was deeply unlikely (the thing was built like a tank) but yet this was not a weekend ride; this was a hard ride into the bush toward the unknown. The only thing he did know was they would be danger.

Brigance walked over to Chambers, acting as if nothing had happened. Brigance gripped the small gun, smoking in his hand. His own gun was back where it belonged.

Chambers put the key in the bike, firing up the engine. He twisted the throttle and the bike revved hard, screaming loud across the countryside, drowning out the sobs from Hanna.

He threw his leg over the bike fitting the helmet to his head, kicking up the side stand. Chambers was ready to go and wanted the drama to end. He needed to go to get away from Hanna and Brigance, to just get away and out into the wild. He could feel it calling to him; the deep dark of the woods of Steel Mountain were before him. The dark trees stood like the jagged teeth of some monster, the woods, the wild; before him, adventure, a fight that appealed to him.

He had been in the army for years and a cop in New York to. The wild, the danger, were to him as important as breathing.

The motorbike's engine was purring softly, Brigance moved over to him, wanting to say something. Chambers want to ride, and Brigance knew this. He put his hand on his forearm, letting this simple and easy act let that be the words.

'Look after the girl. I'll be back in forty-eight hours, one way or the other,' said Chambers.

Brigance nodded, not wanting to cut into Chambers' words.

'If I'm not back in forty-eight hours then I'm not coming back. Take her back to town lie about it, save yourself.'

Brigance looked at Chambers, thinking was this the last time he would ever see him again.

He wanted to punch him in the head, grab the key to the bike, keep him there.

He was his friend, and he was about to leave him, let him go alone in a wild place.

There was a reason they called him the gatekeeper to Steel Mountain: his cabin. His home was the last place of normality; behind that small wood building were those woods, an evil place.

Chambers moved the bike, getting it ready for the off. He looked towards the trees, deep, dark, black giants. He looked at Hanna, still on the ground, childlike.

'Look after the girl,' he whispered.

Brigance nodded. Chambers popped the clutch and Brigance stood back as the bike flew forward, kicking up dirt as it rocketed off at high speed, zooming past Hanna as she sat screaming out a flow of racist hate towards the man who was risking his life to safe her brother.

She watched, calling, shouting, screaming, the tears falling from her eyes as saw the bike enter the trees and then vanish. The sound of the bike faded to nothing... She was alone on the mountain with Brigance and his wife. The tears fell from her eyes but the sobs where gone, and she whispered softly to Chambers, 'Find him... please find him.'

Part Three

'Long is the way and hard,
that out of Hell leads up to Light.'
- John Milton

Chapter One

Fourteen hours' ride or forty-eight hours on foot; that was no good, he had to be back in forty-eight hours. Brigance was no fool and if he told Hanna that he knew or had a very good idea where her brother was then she would put huge pressure on him to call the cops, Brigance was no fool but anyone could make a slip of the tongue and there was the other thought that he could be wrong and they might not be on the miners' path. It was very possible, after all one man buying a lot of food wasn't much to go on, but it was something.

He pushed on harder, his mind burning with a mix of feelings. A large part of him wanted to go back, to be done with Hanna and her lot, but he pushed on, his hand twisting on the bike throttle, popping high on the gears, on the dusty track.

The road was good, but it wouldn't last. Already there were signs that the track was altering. The dirt was getting worse: higher, thick sandy. Of all the things in the world, the motorbike hated sand.

The tyres on the bike were great and made fast work but this wasn't going to be easy. The dirt track was the last sign of man's hand on nature and nature was fighting back. Already the tree branches that hung overhead were reaching out with long, thick, wooden fingers, almost touching him.

He had to move faster. He pushed the bike on, going up the gears, holding the bike at the highest speed he could. The tyres at this speed started to lose grip. The bike kicked left then right. He eased up from his seat, his hands out holding the bike's handle bars, holding them lightly but firmly, standing on the balls of his feet and letting the bike do the work.

It was hot already. The sweat was falling from his brow, getting trapped in his eyes and making them sting. He wished he could move his hand to his face and wipe the sweat away, but he dared not. He had to keep both hands on the bike's handlebars.

He moved his body to left with the path, gently. The bike went to the left and the rear wheel hit a soft pitch of sand. The bike started sliding out of control. He pulled hard at the controls, trying to keep the bike under control. He opened the throttle and the bike screamed, rebalancing its self.

He stood a little higher on the bike's pegs, forearms starting to burn from the effort to keep the bike going.

He had already burnt though an hour. The sun had been high in the sky when he left Hanna and Brigance, but now it was starting to sink, getting closer to the top tree branches, but the heat was getting higher, it felt to him. The heat from the bike was adding to the heat of the mountain; the pipe was getting hot, burning his leg softly but constantly.

The path was covered with fallen tree branches, and they were everywhere. He eased of the gas, pushing his foot down on the rear brake softly, and at once the bike's rear end started to wobble left and right fast, fishtailing.

He held on, lifting his foot off the brake but keeping the gas on the same speed. He started twisting his body this way and that, moving the bike around the fallen wood on the path.

The further he went down the path the worse it become; the path was littered with fallen wood of different sizes, some the size of large matchsticks and others huge chunks of trees. It became impossible to move the bike around all of them. He knew he had to go over some of them.

He gunned the bike, pushing it harder then he should. He knew it too. His mind was on fire. He hit the pieces of trees that he thought the bike could take and the bike smashed into them, bucking up then down.

Chambers' large, powerful body crashed down hard onto the bike's seat. The bike slid out of his control and he was forced to drop his leg down on the sand, kicking the bike up fast, his leg burning with the impact, pain flying though his ankle and thigh.

But there was no choice if he wanted to re-right the bike.

He had to be very careful; if he did that too often then he would injure his ankle, making it impossible to even walk. His mind buzzed, his head ached with just the thought of keep going.

He had to pick which piece of wood to go over and take his chances on that piece of wood; at the speeds he was going it was impossible to see the path, he had to make this own.

He pushed the bike harder as hours passed by. He was taking chances, and the chances were getting bigger and bigger and more dangerous almost to the point where he would lose control of the bike and hurt himself, he could kill himself.

He pushed the bike, forcing this thoughts deep down into his mind, when the bike shot out of his control. The bike's rear wheel locked and bucked out of his control, pulling him away from the bike.

Chambers watched his hands come off and away from the controls. He watched the bike spill away. His hands stayed still, as if he was on the bike. Chambers watched in slow motion as his body left the bike and his hands in mid-air. Fingers closing on nothing, the bike moved away from him, falling hard on its side with an explosion of dust, stones and rocks.

Chambers saw the ground moving fast to hit him. He pushed out his hip, letting his rump take the force of the impact, as that was the largest muscle in the human body. His hand and arm went up and he tucked his head under his bicep and shoulder, protecting his neck. Then he closed his eyes.

The side of ass hit hard into the ground, forcing the air out of his lungs. His body went spinning away, spinning like a top. Chambers pushed his head into his arm, letting that take the force of the crash, closing his eyes, but he couldn't close his mind. The feeling of the world spinning around him was overpowering.

His mind screamed in pain as the world just spun. Then the spinning stopped, as his body slammed down hard into the sandy ground. He bounced then jack-knifed into the sand, rolling, then stopped hard.

He rolled over slowly, moving with great care. His body ached from hitting the ground. He moved upright, sitting on the dirt floor, twitching his legs gently, moving his toes, then calves, then the rest of himself. He was fine; hurt and aching but alive.

He looked over at his bike. It had been through much, much worse. He got to his feet, hitting the kill switch on the bike and the engine cut out, the sound of it echoing around the woods. Then silence filled the large forest.

The stillness hit him just as hard as the falling from the bike. The motionlessness, the quiet, was a sign of danger and his hand moved to his hip, fingers twitching over the gun, eyes raking the large deep shadow filled trees. Nothing happened, nothing at all. But yet it was still there, a feeling of… dread.

Something's out there, his soul told him.

At once his mind moved back to the goal; it overpowered his mind. He had to get the boy.

He walked, a small limp in his leg. He put force down on it as he walked forward and the pain shot up then eased after three steps. He stopped. As he walked around the bike after the ninth step the pain was gone and the limp was almost gone too. He made his way back to the bike.

He grabbed the handlebars, picking up the bike. One hand gripped hard on the handlebars, his other grabbed the side of the seat. Fingers on the steel frame, he dropped his knee under the bike and with a with a great pull and push, he lifted the bike upright.

He looked over both sides of the bike — all seemed fine — then he threw his leg over the bike he clicked the little red kill switch on the bars. He fired up the engine and the bike screamed out as he twisted the gas. He again popped the clutch but more gently this time as he looked down at a wristwatch he had set on one of the handlebars.

It was four p.m. and the sun would set in about three to four hours. He eased the bike around the path, feeling the soft burning pain in his leg as he pushed on. Finding a good rhythm, he moved the bike this way and that; he was in the zone, moving his bike and body as one. He pushed on, building his speed only to have to ease it down, the bike jumping over the wood that still littered the floor. He slammed down hard on the seat and guided the bike around chunks of wood like a downhill skier, moving the bike with shocking ease and speed. He was making good time... but that wouldn't last, and he knew it.

The soft dry, sandy dirt that he was flying over was starting to get thicker and wetter, turning into a thick paste. The bike's tyres were quickly coated in mud, making grip almost impossible. And yet he pushed on harder, the bike skidding around as he fought to keep it under control.

The bike zoomed around, swinging from side to side as he tried to keep the bike upright. He pulled down too hard on the bike and as he did the front wheel hit a piece of wood, jamming in hard.

He shot forward, smashing hard into the ground. He stood fast, moving back to the bike; it was the tenth crash of the day. Again he forced himself back on the bike, body aching, mind aching.

He fell forward in a heap, his face falling into the bars of the bike. He dropped down next to the bike. He took long deep breaths, filling his lungs with sweet air. He wondered how long he could keep going on. Quickly he pulled an energy bar from his pocket, cramming it down his neck as fast as he could, his body greedily taking the much-needed energy.

He re-started the bike, moving down the path, but this time more carefully easing the bike around the path. He came to a sharp bend in the road and as he moved slowly around it, he saw it… a fallen down tree, blocking the whole path, its branches sticking out like the legs of an overturned bug.

He eased the bike closer, trying to work out the best way to go. He sat on the bike looking at the tree, deep in thought. It was way too big to cut though, it would take hours get through it. His eyes raked over the scene trying to work out what was best. The tree had fallen with the last few days too, the leaves where still mostly bright and green; he wondered why it had fallen.

Looking at the stump he saw something. Killing the engine, he moved off the bike to the tree stump. It was covered in large, deep rips and cuts. Someone had cut it down, blocking the whole path. That was a good sign he was on the right path. He guessed the kidnapers had cut it down… made sense. They knew someone was after them.

He looked at the tree. There was no way in hell he was cutting though it or lifting the bike over, so he had to go through the woods.

It should be okay, but he looked at the mud that covered the woodland floor and the edges of dirt path. It was very, very thick there was a good change that the bike would become stuck. He may have to leave the bike, going on foot; that was a thirty-hour hike from here!

'Fuck,' he whispered to no one.

He gunned the bike towards the tree stump, firing the engine hard, the wheels digging in deep into the ground, throwing dirt behind him.

The mud flew up everywhere as he moved around the tree stump pushing the bike, fighting hard to get through the mud, the dirt, throwing the thick mud up behind him.

The mud was thicker here, way thicker. When the tree had been cut down, it had pulled up a lot of dirt with it, throwing it here, there and everywhere. The rain that had fallen a few days ago had turned the shaded area into a mini marsh. The bike fought the mud. The bike was being pulled down into the quicksand-like mud. The rear wheel was sinking and doing it fast, making the front wheel rise up into the air. He pulled and pulled on the gas, feeling the bike sink deeper and deeper into the wet dirt. The rear wheel just spun over and over as the bike went deeper into the ground. The bike's rear wheel got so stuck into the deep mud that it locked.

'No!' said Chambers, spitting out that small and simple word.

The bike cut out. Close to panic, Chambers pushed at the starter button and the bike made odd coughing sounds but nothing seemed to happen. The bike went down further into the mud. He hopped off the bike, knowing his own body weight was pulling the bike deeper into the ground.

As he came off the bike he fell to his knees and the bike went up a little then settled about a half inch. He thought the mud made a strange sucking sound; he watched, he waited. The bike didn't move up at all. It was stuck. And he didn't know if he had the strength to pull it up.

Fuck this mountain! he thought.

His mind on fire, he moved around the bike, thinking hard.

He looked at his watch: 6:32. He had time before the sun went down, but not long.

He stood next to the bike, his pants covered in thick, sticky, mud, making them hard as rock. He grabbed the bars on his bike and started to pull and push at the bike, over and over, until he was red in the face and empty lungs brought him to his knees.

He fell away from the bike, his fingers burning, forearms dull and pain-filled. On the floor, Chambers tried to fill his chest with air. He took a water bottle from his belt, drinking some, his face ruddy, bloodshot eyes popping, resting next to the bike, getting his second wave.

Chambers hadn't realised just how hot he was. He took long deep breaths; thinking hard; he knew what he had to do.

With great effort he forced himself to his feet. Buckling down hard, he put his hand on the bike to re-steady himself.

He was tired. It was only the first day of this and already so much that had happened.

He forced himself up, standing tall; his legs were good for now. He had to get the bike moving, there was no way in hell he could make on foot.

He was on a clock, things were now in motion that couldn't be stopped. Brigance would tell the cops. The last he needed was cops, he knew they would put all of this on him. The kidnapping. Everything. He also knew he couldn't trust Hanna; she would sell him out.

He looked at the woodland floor seeing a large stick laying on the ground. His hand shot out, grabbing the stick and he moved back to the bike using the stick to dig, stabbing it into the ground, pushing the dirt away from the wheels, making a short of trench in the dirt, hoping this would free the bike's tyres.

As he dug, hitting the stick into the wet mud, the stick broke, but he might have done enough to get the bike out. He pulled hard at the mud, with his fingers. His blood was up he wanted out of this place; there was something bad here on the mountain. Cold goosebumps covered his skin with an icy coating of sweat coating his back.

He stood and grabbed the handlebars of the bike, pushing it hard with all his power. Rage covered his features, teeth smashing down on themselves.

The bike moved slowly, then stopped in the mud; he had made little too no progress. He dropped to the underside of the bike. He had an idea. He dug at the mud with his bare hands, pulling great handfuls of mud from under the bike, throwing wet handfuls of mud over his shoulder.

He saw the bike slowly move. It seemed to be working. He had moved the bike's rear wheel and he grabbed at the mud feeling a nail break off. Skin on his fingertip was pulled off and his finger burned, shockwaves of pain shooting though his body; he kept on digging.

A long line of blood dripped from his hands to the forest floor.

He grabbed hard at the mud, pulling and pulling until his muscles screamed out.

The bike's front wheel lowered until it touched the woodland floor. He stood with the last of his strength, started the bike and it came to life. He revved it like a mad man, gently dropping his leg over one side, toes touching the mud.

His legs were wide apart, not sitting on the bike. He let the clutch out, keeping it a low speed with high revs, helping the bike by walking with it as he eased out of the wet muddy area. The bike jammed to stop at the edge of a large oak tree's roots.

Chambers cursed as he pushed, pulled and moved the bike's wheels around the edge of the tree's roots, which looked more like large dark spider's legs reaching out towards him. He edged the bike's wheels around the roots, feeling it move around, almost falling twice, smashing down hard on his legs.

He was free from the roots, but the mud was still there, caked around his wheels; the rear one was getting very bad. Soon the amount of mud would stop the rear wheel from moving at all. But then the ground, the mud, started to get thicker but hard, not as sticky. Chambers could tell as it was easier to move the bike.

The bike started to gain speed, but his body was tired and his eyes closed. The bike jumped, he was of the mud-covered path, he was free.

He shot out of the mud, back onto the hardened dirt and the bike smashed into a large tree branch that Chambers had not seen with his eyes closed. The bike buckled on impact.

He pulled at the bike, keeping it just under control, but then his hand slipped from the gas, stalling the bike.

It shot forward. The bike shot upward then slammed down hard onto the ground. The bike went zigzagging down the hard the dirt road. He grabbed the bike, holding it tight, thumb stabbing the starting button, firing up the bike's engine yet again.

The bike was back under control... but he knew it wouldn't be long before he hit problems again... This was not Steel Mountain. This was hell.

Yet he pushed on for what seemed like miles, passing away from the wet mud, deep into the mountain. Still he was surrounded by thick, dark forest.

His eyes burning with extreme tiredness, he was done. He pulled the bike's rear brake, letting it ease down in speed, looking to his left at the long and seemingly never-ending line of trees.

A small opening in the trees came into view. He slowed down more then pulled the bike into the line of trees going about three hundred yards away from the path. He'd have to make camp and sleep. Tonight he would sleep cowboy style.

He stopped the bike, still sitting on it, keeping it on tick over, looking around the woodland as the sun set and set fast. Long rays of orange light shone through the trees. Random rays of light stabbed into the through the trees as the sun set, so that the trees seemed to be on fire.

He parked, leaning the bike against a large red maple tree. He quickly grabbed dead dry tree branches from the forest floor. Lighting a small fire was a risk, after all, it was the best way of letting an enemy know who where they. But after today he needed that warmth and comfort.

He eased down under the tree, stretching his long powerful body out. He took a mouthful of food and watched the small orange flames growing brighter as the sun set.

He slipped into sleep; it was shockingly easy. The AK-47 was hooked around his right arm and shoulder. The gun dropped softly to the floor of the wood.

Chapter Two

Nights on mountains were always dark, even in the high summer. The dark sometimes seemed to be painted over your eyes, as if nature was forcing a mask over your face, keeping its nocturnal activities a dark secret from man's eyes. That was why Chambers loved a fire, even though he was well aware that it was a great way to let anyone who wanted you dead, know you were there.

A fire was a sign saying, "I'm here, come get me!"

But he liked it. He was not fond of the dark, even though in his time it had been his best friend. Still, it was a friend one should always keep a very close eye on.

He was sleeping a "sleep with one eye open". He called it sleeping in halfs. He was asleep, but his mind was close to the edge, ready to wake when needed. He lay on his back, his baseball cap lowed, his hands across his belly, his feet and legs stretched next to the flames.

In his half asleep his mind registered the sound first, but it took a long time for the sound too wake him.

It was the sound of a paw being put down on the woodland floor gently, as if something were hunting him. The thing with the paws could smell something. Its small brain had nowhere near the power of its nose, but its nose had done its job. It had smelled food, and the best food, something that could bleed. There were small, tiny traces of blood in the air; on the woodland floor.

That great black bear had smelled it. The bear didn't understand how the small drops of blood could be spread across a large amount of land. A deer maybe? Injured, running fast?

The blood was small yet there. The bear pushed its large wet snout down into the leaves and mud, losing the smell, then finding it.

The bear was hunting, and hunting something that it could eat. The bear knew the thing it was hunting was injured; it had been bleeding and going this way.

The bear had zero idea of what a motorbike was. But the bear was confused how it moved so far with an injury. But it cared it was bleeding and therefore it could be eaten.

But the bear had seen injured deer move so fast even with great, and to the bear, delicious looking wounds.

So the bear assumed that a deer or some other fast-moving prey was close and injured. If the bear could sneak up on it, then the bear would have a good meaty, blood-filled meal.

The bear wandered down the muddy path that led too Chambers, smelled his blood.

The same bloody nightmare path that Chambers had fought so hard on, to the bear it was nothing. The bear moved over the muddy path as if it was nothing more than just dirt.

The bear's powerful body walked over the dry sticks, which snapped loud enough to enter Chambers' mind. It warned him and woke him.

He woke softly but completely. At first he didn't know why he had woken. His eyes flashing open saw nothing in the dim night. The fire, a large orange flower when he'd last seen it, was now a few dark red glowing embers.

The moon was covered by clouds, so no hope of moonlight. He blinked trying to force his eyes to work in the gloom.

His hand moved slowly towards his AK-47 gently picking it up.

The gun moved with a small rustle from the strap and a soft metallic thud from the gun as he rested it on leg. His other hand moved to the handle and trigger. He tried to keep his movements slow. He thought — no, he *knew* — it was a bear, behind him.

The bear's powerful snout could smell it: the softly dropping blood fall from the prey. Its bright eyes shone in the dark, watching the tree line trying to see the prey.

Then the bear stopped, its body ready to attack, but *it* (the prey) had moved. The bear's body language changed from a pure attack to a defensive style of attack. The first thing had happened through its powerful muzzle. A collection of new smells had crashed into its nose, alighting its senses. It smelled mud, dirt and death. The bear sniffed at the crisp air; it smelled the blood that it had been hunting for a while, but there was something else, a new smell, softer.

Blood and mud were nothing new to the bear, no it had smelled something else, a new smell and a smell that it had smelled many, many times before. The bear had marked that smell in his mind as dangerous, the smell of metal. It was a smell it was used too even here on Steel Mountain. But this was different, the smell of this metal, meant only one thing: man. The bear associated that smell with one thing: danger. The dark metal smell, a heavy smell of gun metal.

It was a smell that bear hated. It hated the smell of gun metal and the burning powder smell that hung in the air.

The bear remembered its brother, years ago, when it was a cub in its litter. The two of them came across a stranger, and the stranger had made that odd bright human flower, fire. The two bears at that time had never seen fire before and it was something else. Something new, magical.

The two young bears had moved towards it, almost dancing around the flower, watching it, testing it. When its sibling moved too close to the powerful flower, the bear had begun to scream with great powerful cries. It had watched its sibling scream as its dark black fair became a fireball, its skin burning and melting off its back, the bear running around in crazy circles.

It screamed at its sibling, confused as to what to do and what was happening, when its sibling ran too close. The bear threw one of its paws at the burning bear, twice hitting it with powerful blows, feeling the power of that red flower, as the flames burnt though its fur too.

That was when it ran from its burning sibling. It never saw its sibling again, but it remembered the smell of the burning, locked deep into its mind. The same way a vicious act will locked into the mind of a human.

The bear smelled that red flower and the gun metal that hunters used. But it also smelled blood and not only blood but sweat and heat from the prey.

The meal was close. It had been a long time since the bear had eaten flesh and it needed it. But the bear was smart (as far as it could be). This was not going to be an easy fight.

This food wouldn't just run it. It would fight and it had mastered that red orange burning, poisonous flower.

The bear lowered itself down looking hard at the place where it knew the meal was.

It saw it, next to a tree. The tree trunk blocked the meal from the bear's eyes. But its nose smelled it and smell was enough, it was by that tree. the bear moved slowly and carefully, its front left paw down on the ground.

The bear's head shot to the right, looking. It could see it, it could smell it the red flower. It was almost dead. But the meal was life and as injured as it had thought.
The bear's mind flowed back with memories of its sibling burning in front of its eyes. The smell of that red flower was burnt into its mind; it could see and smell the fire.

The bear relaxed. The red, burning flower was low. Only a tiny sparking thing that couldn't hurt it, could it?

What about the gun metal? That could kill the bear. The fact that smell could kill was what mattered, yet all things it hunted had something to fight back with.

The fish could go deeper into the water than the bear could. The deer were faster than a bear and the buck had large and strong antlers that it could slam into its body. The bear paused, thinking.

It had tasted all the flesh of those things, but this one, this was a new smell; it had never had human before.

It would attack. But how? A head on attack? Or a silent attack on the thing? It moved slowly around the tree, taking its time.

It's a deer, thought Chambers, more in hope than reason. *A bear would have attacked by now*. But still, what if it wasn't?

He pulled the bolt of the rifle back as far it would go. It clicked, letting him know it was ready. His thumb also moved fast to the safety catch, which he turned off, and his finger moved to the selector. He had three choices: one shot, three shots or fully automatic.

He clicked the three shot on the selector of the AK-47, still thinking, *It's a deer*. He wished he could believe that it was a deer and just close his eyes and sleep. Instead he kept the gun in his hands, his hands already slick with sweat.

He heard it, the sound he knew all too well: the growl of a bear.

A bear, a black bear most likely, was close behind him. It would attack soon. He knew this for a fact.

His baseball cap covered his eyes, blocking his vison as well as the dark night.

Shit! He thought he needed to take it off. But he was afraid that his movement would excite the bear. If he were to be attacked it wouldn't be for removing his fucking hat.

He eased the gun, moving it to his chest.

Move the gun slowly, he said to himself in his mind. But not slow enough not to be useful, if the bear attacked. This was hard. And his heart was reacting to the stress; his heartbeats were getting faster and harder hammering inside in his chest so loudly, that the bear could, most surely, hear his heart.

Could the bear hear it? The sound would excite the bear into madness. The bear was close, he could feel it, in the small sounds around him. The stillness from the other animals in the wood, all were gone. They knew to stay away from a hunting bear.

He eased the AK-47 from his side. It was ready; he hoped he would be. He listened hard; the bear was growling; it could hear him, smell and see him. Chambers felt what it was to be hunted.

The bear was ready. It wondered if its prey was readying to fight back? The bear made up its mind and attacked. The bear paws crashed down hard, jet black, dirty claws came from the paws.

Chambers now knew where the bear was, to his left. *I must be quick*, was his last thought.

In one quick motion, he jumped to his feet, feeling his leg bones burning after hours of laying on the cold ground.

His right hand shot to his head, slapping off the baseball cap. His hand over his eyes, he couldn't see for what seemed like an eternity.

He threw that hand down back on the stock of the gun, fingers zooming towards the trigger.

His other hand shot out to the barrel of the gun, catching the small blue light that was on the end; he pressed it and a bright blue-white light flashed on, illuminating the dark wood.

He pointed the rifle at the spot he thought the bear was, without knowing for sure. He was ready to fire, but he saw nothing, just the dark line of trees. He moved down, his body low, his heart screaming inside his chest, the blood boiling and pumping around his body, teeth closed down hard, his jaw a tight line.

He looked out across the woods knowing the bear was close, moving the rifle around the woodlands, searching. Then he heard the roar of the bear. He spun and the bright white light of the AK-47 hit the bear.

The bear was there, jumping out in the harsh light, its mouth open, large, wet, yellow teeth bared.

He fired at it, the rifle kicking, shaking. He was not balanced. Falling to his side, he hit the ground and kept on firing.

The bullets hit the bear, bullets flying though the bear's fur, taking out large chunks of skin and flesh.

The bear growled with pain, storming away. Smoke rose from the bullet holes. It was blind with pain and rage. The bear ran hard, fast. It turned back towards its meal, roaring at the top of its lungs. It was more than a meal; it was a fight.

Chambers moved the rifle around the woods, the light shining through the trees, looking for the bear. He moved his back to the tree, using it as some protection. The bear was hunting him silently.

He needed to know where the damn fucking thing was. Taking in deep breaths, he tried to get himself under control. His eyes raked the line of trees, seeing nothing, hearing nothing.

But he knew it was out there.

He moved from the tree. The icy blue-white light showed him nothing but trees. He looked deeper into the tree; little did he know but the bear had moved around him.

Chambers heard it, spinning on the spot, his finger on the trigger, pulling it over and over before he had even seen the bear, or turned fully.

The bear was lit up in the glow of the gun's light. As he fired at the bear, it jumped towards him its claws out, mouth open and it roared

He let the AK scream out. The bullets slammed into the bear's head and neck. The large bullet slammed into the bear's neck, breaking it, killing it almost at once.

Chambers threw himself out of the way of the dead yet still charging bear. Its corpse weighed over a ton and it was coming straight at him.

With a yell, still not sure if the beast was dead or not, Chambers jumped away, hitting hard into the woodland floor, rolling over.

He came to stop at once. He was on his knees holding the Ak-47 in his arms, pointing the gun at the dead bear. His heart was racing, his breath coming in short sharp breaths, dirt falling from his hair and face.

He stood, aiming the rile at the bear.

He waited to see if the bear moved. Chambers didn't know if it was dead or not.

He clicked the AK-47 from three shots to one.

He moved slowly towards the bear; this thing was big. With one swipe of its paw it could and would cut his head off.

He crept forward, placing the rifle close to the bear's head. Getting as close as he dared, he pulled once on the trigger.

The shot sounded amazingly loud in the deep still woods, echoing around, letting the whole mountain know he was there.

Smoke rose from the barrel; smoke rose from the gunshot in the bear's head, its freshly dead blood cooling in the night. A small column of smoke went up from the bear's head, almost like a soul.

Time to go! he thought.

No more sleep for Chambers.

He grabbed his stuff, firing the bike up, its tail light vanishing into the woods with the call of the engine. The bear's body was still in death.

Chapter Three

He pushed the bike on hard, watching the long shadows reach out towards him as the bright orange-red sun burnt its way across the mountain as it rose. Long thin shifts of golden light lit up the way, as Chambers pushed on, the bike's engine calling out as he went.

He pushed the bike though mud and a rough path. The tree line was farther back now, as he pushed on past and though the tree lines, until there were hardly any trees. But this was Steel Mountain; one problem replaced another.

Boulders — large ugly, grey, moss-covered ones, sharp as razors — littered the path ahead. To the right and left of him there was a large grey cliff like wall around him.

He pushed on, going slowly then faster. The size of the boulders set the speed he could go. One was so big he had to stop and walk the bike around it, and that started happening over and over.

Twice he fell, crashing down hard into the stony floor, missing the razor shape rocks by inches, body aching taking hit after hit.

The bike's wheels crunched over thousands of pebbles that covered the ground. This had Chambers concerned, as not only were there small stones but they were getting wet. And that meant one thing: water, lot of water, a river.

When the boulders eased, he jumped back on the bike, driving through, around and over the rocks, but too fast. The rear wheel hit something kicking out; the front wheel was out of control. His eyes went wide as he fought to keep the bike under control, arms hanging on for dear life, white hot shots of pain whizzing up and down his arms, starting from his forearms then flying from his shoulders. He slammed his legs closed on the bike trying with powerful thighs to keep the bike under his control, but it was too late; the bike's front smashed into a boulder.

He flipped over the bars, head first, hands waving, trying to defend his head then... he smashed down into the rocks.

Chambers just flipped his body forward, saving himself from jack knifing into the hard, cold, cruel rocks and instead he hit back first.

Body hit hard; he was stretched out on the rocks. He waited, testing his body, searching though the different levels of pain to see how badly his body was hurt. All seemed okay. He was stunned, but not broken.

He stood very slowly, his head aching, body cold and stiff.

He pulled the bike up, taking off his helmet. He'd have to walk the bike from now on. His vison went bright red. Pain shot though him. His vison went deep and dark, until the darkness seemed to cover his eyes. He fell forward, smashing into the bike. His crash helmet went flying. He landed in a heap but this time right onto a large rock. One of his legs shot out, shaking in pain. His back went tight with the pain flying though him.

He was in shock with the force of two crashes coming so close and other things, everything in his mind started to crash down, like a virus filled computer.

The fight with the bear, the kid, the search… hell, his life; the last years seemed to hit him all at once… as he blacked out.

Chambers' body fell to the side. The sound of the bike's engine filled the side of the mountain then died. The rear wheel spun a few times, then stopped. The mountain returned to its true way, a place where man was small, where humans had no business.

Chambers was on his side lying next to the bike. He moved in his passed-out sleep. As he did he slipped down to the right, falling hard. A sharp rock smashed hard into his face, cutting him. A deep pool of blood ran down his face.

The rock cut deeper into his face, as his head rested more on the rock. The pain shot into his mind, waking him.

His mouth opened; he bellowed loud and deep, the scream cutting the inside of his throat, ringing across the rocks and boulders that covered the path up the mountain.

He pulled himself up and his hand went to his face, feeling blood ooze from his between his fingers.

The cracks in his mind started to show. He fell to his knees, rage blowing up inside his mind. He started hitting his hands down hard on the stone floor, while yelling over and over.

'Mistake, after mistake, after mistake,' he screamed. It was a mix of two things: pain and frustration.

He clawed himself back to his feet, his head spinning. The world was spinning around, making him dry heave. He had stop it, closing his eyes tight, he reopened his eyes. The world didn't stop spinning. He reclosed them even tighter, holding on, trying to force his body and mind to heal.

Gently and slowly he reopened his eyes. The world was spinning but slower. He tried to take a step but when he did his eyes widened, his neck burnt and he throw up. Then he fell to his knees.

The words he had spoken were echoing in his mind. 'Mistake, after mistake, after mistake.'

He pulled himself across to a large rock and sitting on it, he lowered his head down between his knees, taking in deep long breaths.

He had to get a grip, he had to get control; if he kept this up he was a dead man.

He pulled out some water, taking a deep but controlled drink of it, replacing the lid.

He needed to take it easy. He took out his cell phone, placing the camera on selfie. The cut was deep but he thought he could get by without stitches, until he got of this mother fucker of a mountain.

From the bike's side panel he took his first aid kit and found a large plaster and an alcohol wipe.

He balled the wipe around his finger, jabbing it in the cut. A fire of pain went from his face to his brain which lit it up with pure pain.

His hand turned into a ball becoming a claw, fingers cutting into the flesh of his thigh.

But the pain in his face and head... eased. Quickly he pulled the plaster and. using his image in the cell phone, he put the plaster on.

He stood; the world seemed fine and he felt okay. His leg had taken the worst of it after his face. He'd have to check that too.

Opening his pants he pulled them down and he looked at his leg, letting out a shocked gasp. On his upper thigh was a nasty looking purple-red mark going from hip to kneecap, oozing blood. It was bad, but not the end of the world. He pulled this pants back up, moving carefully around the rocks, testing his leg and body, looking for any sign that his body was not working. His leg hurt but he could work with it. He walked around in small rings, putting as much weight on his leg as he thought was safe, testing it. If he couldn't walk, that was it. It would be his life that would be in danger, and he'd have to run from the mountain. His mind and body hurt so much... but it was workable.

He moved to the bike, grabbing it, forcing the bike upright.

It made some truly shocking sounds as the metal grated on the dangerous rocks. He eased slowly onto the bike, testing his leg, hoping it could take the position he needed to ride.

He fired the bike up, for what seemed like the thousandth time, the bike started.

He eased the bike forward, keeping it at such a low speed that he knew that he could walk faster than this and more safely, but if he walked he couldn't take the bike with him and it would have been too hard.

He looked ahead, seeing the large rocks change in size, getting smaller. He was close to leaving this boulder field.

The boulder field was going, but it was not gone, and it would not go without a fight. He still had to go easy, fighting the bike, fighting the boulders and rocks, as he moved the bike on and on.

Then he saw it, a forest. He wondered if it was the same forest he fought the bear in. Broken up by the boulders.

He eased the bike out of the boulder field. He looked up at the forest in front of him. He twisted down hard on the bike's gas, shooting into the depths. Within seconds there was no sign that the boulder field had ever been there. It felt as if, and maybe it was, the mountain was testing him.

Chambers and his bike flew though the treeline, a maze of colours of browns and greens, as he eased the bike around the path. It was good going; but he knew it wouldn't last. And it didn't he heard it way before he saw it.

He didn't want to hear it as he knew what it was. His mind tried to block out the truth, but he knew. He knew damn well what it was.

He pushed on, pushing the bike hard. His head would shoot down from time to time, looking at the bike's gauges. His fuel was getting lower. He'd have to top it up.

He pressed down on the brakes, the bike easing to a stop.

Chambers moved off the bike, looking around, his eyes digging into the rows and rows of trees that stood around him. The danger was there, it was right there, in the woods and hills that towered around him.

Without thinking his hands moved, his black gloved fingers touching the wood and steel of the rifle. His fingers moved away from the gun as he the felt the woods stare back at him.

He had to focus on the task at hand. He took the keys from the bike, opening the fuel cap and unhooking the gas can from the bike's rack.

He undid the lid, pouring the liquid into the bike's tank, wishing that gravity would move faster, that the amber liquid would fall faster in his tank.

The gas can was empty and he thought about retying the can onto the bike's rack. Then, looking around, he tossed the green metal can far as he could, watching it arc into the air then crash down into the vegetation.

A cloud of birds shot out from the line of trees, flying up into the air, signalling to the other birds and beasts on this mountain that he was here, that danger was here.

The sound he knew all too well was roaring into his ears. But he hoped with all his might that he was wrong but he knew he wasn't.

He had known he would come across it, but he had hoped it would not be as bad as he knows it's going to be.

The sound gave it away. In fact it could be the end of the line.

Something moved in the woods to the side of him. His mind stopped thinking about anything else; all of his powers and senses where now focused on that movement.

His body dropped down low to one knee, his hand pulling the AK-47 over his body, so now it was resting on his hip. One hand went to the trigger, fingers wrapped around it; the gun was ready to fight.

He watched, eyes burning, the line of trees looking for something, anything. Nothing moved.

After a while, what seemed like hours, he moved upright, standing, body tight, eyes blazing, a dull fear inside him as he moved back to the bike. He threw his leg over it.

He fired it up, flying down hard into the grey dusty road, leaving a falling mist of powder in the air behind his rear wheel.

It didn't take long, no time at all before the sound wasn't deafening but overpowering. He came over a small rise in the road, seeing small glimpses of it.

It was greyer then blue, the river. He hit the bike's brakes, coming to a skidding stop. The dust came up from the road around his legs. His face was a grim mask of rage, as he looked at the iron-coloured river.

Bright white foam on the shockingly fast-moving river's waves crashed viciously into the rocks. He watched the great waves that flowed down the river, only to see them break, flying apart as the wave smashed into rocks.

Chambers sat on the saddle of the bike. He didn't know what to do next. There was no way he was making it across on the bike. It was too high and too fast. The bike would be pushed over in a flash, most likely trapping him under it, then he would drown.

Could he make on foot? he thought as he looked at the river. It was fast, deep and wide, moving, always moving in great waves.

Water was being dropped down hard from the melting snow and ice, from high up on the mountain's peak.

This river shouldn't be like this, it was normally a third smaller. But the river was huge. Chambers watched the cruel looking water.

He saw a great chunk of the bank drop off into the waters below.

He kicked down hard on the ground wondering what the hell was he going to do. There was no way the bike was going to make it; even if the river wasn't that fast he would drown the bike. He needed the bike to work if he was ever going to get that kid and himself of this mountain, but for the bike this was the end of the line, until the return journey.

Stepping off the bike he let it stall. He dropped the bike's side stand. He walked closer to the river, his eyes glued on the iron-grey water smashing and crashing around itself, hearing its deafening screams.

He looked down at the water wondering if he could make it across. Could he do it on foot? Maybe.

He looked back to the bike behind him, he would have to hide it in the woods. He looked to his right at the trees.

He could move the bike into those woods. He moved to the bike, starting it up, riding into the woods, around two hundred and fifty yards, into the bush, looking around for somewhere to hide the bike. He saw a large deep bush overgrown with a large tree behind it. *Perfect*, he thought with a smile.

He dropped the bike to its side, and gently he half pushed and half wiggled the bike under the bush.

It was hard, hot work. Already there was a thick layer of hot salty sweat that covered his face, hands, armpits and groin. He could feel his skin bubbling, dark raw red patches between his legs were appearing.

He fought on with the bike, resting it on its side. The bush had hard and cruel thorns; he felt the thorns cutting deep into his flesh.

His facial muscles made small jumping motions as the wet salty sweat and thorn cuts met. To hell with this place! The bike was on its side and covered; he slipped his crash helmet next to the bike, no point taking it with him.

He looked at it. That bike and he had been all over this state; it was a sad thing but his truck and bike, were things he bonded with, his friends.

He had no friends, or family. He looked down at the bike under the bush. It looked more like a loyal dog to him, than plastic, steel and iron.

With a heavy heart he pushed the thoughts away. It was a bike and if it got damaged then Hanna's rich, woke, brat parents would pay, one way or the other.

He grabbed rough, knobbly sticks that littered the floor of the woodland, throwing them over the bike, camouflaging it from view. With one last look at the bike he ran back (as best he could) to the path, never knowing if he would see it again.

At the river's edge, his mind spinning, he wondered what his best options where. The water was even faster here, moving at great speed, fantastic waves crashing over and over one another. He stood on the edge of the river, with his mind racing. But with each racing thought only three options came to mind, and all were bad.

He could walk it, raft it or go back. That was it and only it.

He knew that the last one was the one he should do. The kid was dead. He been dead for a long time as well. Of that he was still sure. And yet here he stood, boots getting wet.

He was sure he was dead killed within hours off his taking. He knew that it had to be the case. Why the hell would they keep him alive?

Maybe just maybe he'd be alive, he thought. Hell, the kidnappers could do a fair trade, money for the kid. He could be alive. But he knew better, that kid was dead.

He knew he was tracking nothing more than a dead body. That was his expectation; his hope was something else — that the boy would be alive. Then he reminded himself, hope is for the weak.

Standing on the water's edge, watching the rapid waters screaming down and across the mountain, cutting though the side of Steel Mountain itself, he eased forward, dropping his right foot into the icy water, testing the water and his clothes. Even through his thick, brown leather boot, he felt the fast, strong water. It was colder than ice.

This is what death must feel like, he thought.

Death was something he knew about. He had killed more men than most serial killers, but all his kills had been lawful, even the one that ruined his life. That had been a lawful kill, but as it turned out it was an immoral kill. He was just given the wrong information.

Don't think about that, his mind shot at him.

An image in his mind's eye: a dead black man in the street, fresh red bullet holes covering his chest, his hand on the gun, the river seemed to fade.

The wild was lost to him, he saw it… New York. He saw his SWAT police outfit. The second he heard it though the radio. The worst words he had ever heard in his life.

'Wrong man, don't fire… repeat, don't fire.'

He had ready killed him.

Another white cop who killed a black man. He may as well have shot himself too. But he had done the right thing.

'*No!*' he yelled. 'Not now!'

He returned to the now. New York faded, the dead man on the floor faded. Maybe, just maybe, this case would wash that death clean? Maybe.

Looking down he saw the water pushed hard over his foot. Flying over his legs, the water going up his body.

The power of the river actually moved his foot making him fall backwards; he quickly rebalanced. There was no way he could just walk across, and he didn't have the time or tools to build a raft.

He swore, spitting into the river in anger. He needed to get over that river. Looking down at the ground he saw dozens of sticks. But all too small, he needed something like a staff to help him walk across the river, but there was nothing over two foot long.

Then he saw a long branch reaching out from icy water. It looked strong. Grabbing it with both hands like King Arthur most have done with Excalibur, he pulled it with all his strength. The stick was more like a tree limb, it groaned from the pressure he was putting on it.

The stick stayed strong, trapped under a large rock. A good sized one too, by the feel of it. It felt like something strong was under the waves hanging onto the stick, stopping him from pulling it free and moving on with his journey.

He looked at the deep iron-grey waters and felt it, the evil that was in this place, the overpowering feeling that something wasn't right.

It was this place, this mountain, Steel Mountain. It was a bad place; it was in the rocks, the water, the trees; the very air here was not normal. He could feel it in his soul.

They should burn it to the ground, he thought *run a holy fire of napalm on this mountain and watch it burn!*

He watched as the grey water smashed hard into the large boulders that stood high in the riverbed. The riverbed was invisible under the carpet of iron-grey water.

With a groan he pulled at the stick, his jaw locked, eyes popping, muscles screaming and then... then the stick broke. But it broke at the bottom of the boulder. The stick came free, and even broken it stood at almost six foot tall.

He stood, the ice water lapping over his brown boots, deep in thought. He had to make his mind up, was he going yes or no. He knew the answer.

He took the first step in the river. Now both feet were under the ice water. He waded into the almost frozen river, using the stick to help him.

He walked further into the ice water and moved quickly, stabbing the tree limb into the iron ice water, pushing forward even as the water crashed around his feet. It was hard going, and he knew it would get worse.

The water crashed over his thighs now.

He was not even halfway across the river.

He kept moving forward, his pants sticking to his legs, as he took large steps, trying to keep moving in the water, boots trying to grip the rocky riverbed, with not much success: he tripped twice, the first time he went down to his chest.

His clothes at once became waterlogged, pulling him closer to the deep waves. Chambers hopped up, forcing himself out of the ice water.

The second time he slipped and went down back first into the ice water, but this time his head and face went under the dark water.

The bright blue sky was lost to him under the grey waters. Thank God for the stick, he stabbed it down hard into the rocks, pulling himself with all his might and broke out of the ice water. Spitting the freezing waters, a yell escaped from blue, grey lips. And he pushed on.

He had to stop several times, knifing the stick deeper into the river trying to check the depth of the fast-moving water.

He was halfway across now, the water up too his midriff. He turned sideways into the crashing waves that smashed into his body. The stinging water crashed into his eyes, blinding him for a second or two. He blinked out the water, eyes burning, then sight retuned.

Moving like a crab he crossed the river, the water now smashing around his lower chest. He somehow manged to stay on his feet, the cold of the water taking his breath away. His body temperature had dropped like a stone; his breath came in short hard breaths.

The water hit him hard, so hard that it felt more like punches then water.

The water went into his open mouth, taking more air away from him. He moved, still going sideways; he had better footing this way.

He glanced to the other side of the river bank; it looked as far from him as far as the moon.

He kept on his crab like walking then it happened: his foot slipped on rock. He tried to rebalance himself with the stick, jamming it down hard. But it was hopeless. The stick shot from his hands. He gasped as his heavy muscled frame smashed down hard into the grey water.

A wave hit him, sending him flying through the water, as another small wave smashed into the spot he had been making a small ring of white foam. The stick he had been using now floated by, the stick and the foam from his fall the only signs he had ever been in that river.

The long, strong, stick that he had been using gently floated on the water then that it too went under as a wave smashed into it. There was no sign that he, Chambers had ever even seen this river.

But Chambers was there, he was just under the water.

The river was pulling him faster and deeper. His clothes, heavy and waterlogged, weighed him deeper into the river. The waves tossed him around.

His eyes were wide open as he saw the large rocks on the bottom of the river bed. The rocks zoomed close to his head, as waves hurled him towards the bottom. He threw up his arm trying to protect his head as he shot towards the rocks.

His right arm and hand smashed into the knife-like rocks and great chunks of skin and flesh were ripped from his body.

His scream was lost in the water. Only a line of bubbles went into the water and up to the air.

The water flipped his body over and over until he was not sure where up was and where down was.

As he spun in the water he tried to swim up but there was no hope. Every time he pulled with his powerful arms and legs, about to break though the water to the sweet air, he was pulled back from it by a powerful wave, his powerful body being thrown deeper into the water.

In these waters he was nothing more than a small rock in the roaring river.

He pushed on hard towards the surface, the grey, dirty, water choking him, filling his lungs and brain.

He made a mad dash for the sweet air, limbs screaming, heart racing, muscles ripping.

He was so close to the sweet fresh air.

He screamed under the waves; He pushed with all his might; his fingers broke the roaring surface, his head crashing though the water, stealing great lungsful of air. But only for a blissful few seconds. Then a great wave smashed into his chest, and he was pulled back into the iron grey coloured water.

He shot up for a few seconds then with a small splash he had vanished under the waves.

He had to think and do it fast. If he didn't get this under his control then he would drown in this fucking river. He fought hard with the river, only to be pushed around by the fast-moving waves.

This is hell, thought Chambers.

He was too heavy, his clothes too waterlogged, he was going deeper. He would have to do something, anything.

He kicked hard only to have his body burst out of the water for a second then just go back in to freezing waters' depths. He had to find a way to get out of the water. If he only a life jacket.

Think, think... fucking think, he screamed inside his mind. *Think or die.*

Then he remembered something he had read about, a man in the navy who had fallen overboard into the sea. He had made a life jacket out of...

His hand went towards the knife, pulling it from his belt. The water crashed around him and into him, almost knocking the blade from hands before he fully pulled it out.

He held on tighter to the handle of the blade, his fingers turning white. This was his life line. He started to kick hard at his tight boots but they didn't move, the water still throwing him around like a rag doll. As his body hit the rocky floor of the river bed, forcing the air from lungs, he breathed in, a natural act, but he was under the waves. His lungs filled with water as it went inside him. He held on, trying not to breathe again.

He pulled his right leg to him, stabbing the blade into the top of his boot. He felt the tip of the blade stab into the tongue of the boot. He jabbed it down, cutting though the boot laces. He cut and pushed his blade down, watching the boot laces rise up before him in the water; then with the other foot he kicked hard at the loose boot and it came off, flying away from him in the water. He turned the knife to the other foot.

His head burnt with pain. He was fighting hard; his mind and soul screamed out air. He had to get air know.

He pushed hard with his arms, kicking with his legs. His head was about to break the surface of the water, then

145

the water pulled him back. It was if there were hands underneath pulling him back down under the waves, back into the choking dark waters.

He pulled harder. His face broke the water but only his face; he spat out the water from his lungs, and taking a quick breath he went back under.

He turned his body around, his hand still holding tightly to the knife. He jibbed the blade down into his other boot, cutting at the laces. This time it was much harder as the water was trying to roll him over and over.

He fought hard with the water, Stabbing the knife deeper into the boot going in too far, cutting into the flesh of his foot.

A small cloud of blood bloomed towards him.

He wanted to scream then slammed his mouth shut.

He held on to his air as best he could, fighting the pain that was screaming inside of him. He pulled out the knife from his foot, a cry inside his mind, invisible tears rolling down his face. He stabbed down into his boot again, cutting through the boot laces; more laces came off to float past him.

He kicked out hard into his foot; the boot moved, coming off his foot, but got stuck at his heel.

His body flipped again in the river, and Chambers kicked out, he missed his boot, his foot smashing into his calf, then again he kicked. This time he smashed the boot with his heel.

The boot went off, flying over and over; within a second the boot was lost in the speed of the river.

He fought against the power of the river as it spun him around. He popped up for a second trying to breath. But he was under before he could take a breath. The water crashed around him, deafening, the waves crashing around him pulling him under, pushing him down.

The sound of the water was filling his ears until the only thing he could hear was the sound of the water; he wondered if he lived would the water deafen him.

Chambers' hands went to his belt, he dropped the knife seeing it disappear into the fast-moving ice iron waters. He popped open his belt; next his fingers started pulling at the button and the zipper. The pants where undone. He kicked and pulled them off.

The shock of the icy water crashed into his bare legs, taking away what little breath he had.

He pulled the pants from his body, holding them tight. He had to work fast as fast as the river, cold hands moving to the leg ends of the pants, tying a knot in them. First the right one, then the left. It was hard to use his hands in the icy water that just kept smashing into him.

Chambers' body sank into the ice water as another wave hammered over him. He looked up towards the air, as the water dragged him away from the sweet air, the sweet, soft, life-giving air.

This was his one and only chance, and he kicked hard towards the surface holding his pants close to his chest, the waistband clamped down tight, making sure no water got in. He pushed hard, keeping the pants clamped to his chest, as he fought hard, kicking, pulling, jumping towards the air.

He shot out of the water. But it was not air he was after, well not for his lungs, the air was for his pants. He pulled the pants up and out letting them meet the air, like airing out a bedsheet. Air crashed into the wet pants, the knots in the legs blocking its escape.

When the legs of the pants were filled with air, ballooning out, his hands slammed down hard pining the waist of the pants shut tight, forcing the air to stay in.

The legs were filled with air. He then clamped the air-filled pants to his chest using his wet pants as life jacket. It worked; the air-filled pants made him float on the icy water.

He shot down stream holding on tight to his pants-come-life-jacket. He breathed in tight thick lungsful of air. His mind started to work again, thank God for air.

He didn't move, just clung onto the pants, letting the water take him where it went.

He was breathing hard, the colour coming back to his face.

He looked across the river bank, looking for somewhere to go. But the river was moving too fast for him to do anything. But he had to make a move, he felt the freezing water working on his body. His face was turning blue. If he didn't drown he would freeze.

He kicked like mad, letting the water help him, moving with the waves to reach the edge of the bank. Twice he almost made it, and twice the fast-moving waves smashed him away just when he thought he was about to escape.

His body crashed into the bank of the river; he flung out a hand, fingers clawing into the wet mud, only to be pulled past by the speed of the roaring river.

He knew that soon his body temperature would drop down very low, too low; soon he would die. His eyes raked the riverbank looking for something; he saw it, an opening, very small, just a blip sticking out into the river. That was his lifeline.

He pressed his body down hard, smashing himself into lip, the bank of the river, jamming himself there. His body slammed into the wet sandy mud. His shoulder screamed out in pain from the impact. He jammed his jaws down hard, stopping the scream that was aching to escape his mouth.

Coughing up a mix of dirty ice water and blood, he hit the bank and stopped moving in the water, the rough, rocky sand cutting into his back and bare legs, blood blooming around him, as the water pressed him to the bank's lip.

The water pushed him off the side of the bank.

One of his hands shot out towards the sandy bank, fingers stabbing claw-like into the sand. With a roar he pulled himself against the flow of the river, his other hand still holding on to his pants stabbed into the sandy mud too. He pushed hard and his lower body came up and out of the waves. His hands scrambled on the mud, as his body slammed down hard onto the earth, into the wet and sticking mud.

His naked legs were pulled from the water. He was free. He twisted himself onto the safety of the earth, he kicked at the water, his bare legs touching wet mud. He moved snake like in the mud, away from the iron-grey water. His body was beaten. But at least he was out the fast-moving ice water. And he was alive and on the right side of the bank.

He moved on his hands and knees then he fell down hard into the wet, light mud of the bank.

He rolled over, looking up at the sky framed in tree branches as he coughed up water from his chest.

He sat up, looking down at his bare legs, tracks of blood running down them from the thousand cuts from the rocks.

He took the AK-47 from his back, looking over it. A drop in the water was nothing to his gun; but he quickly broke it down, draining the water out of the rifle.

The two pistols as well, he took as much water as he could out of them. The AK would be okay, but the pistols he wasn't sure about.

He took the Magnum, breaking that down too, removing as much water from it as he could.

He held the gun in his hands, pulled back the hammer aiming the gun into the air; he pulled the trigger. The gun kicked, loud and long.

The shot went booming around the trees. But the sound of the gun was lost in the roar of water.

He placed the Magnum down on the ground; taking the Storm Beretta pistol he did the same; it clicked, he pulled it again. Nothing happened so he broke the gun down again.

Looking inside it, he saw a great mound of mud inside the gun, was it broken?

Pissed, Chambers put his little finger inside, pulling at the mud, digging it out. His finger shook from the cold and wet. The mud stayed put. Looking around he saw a long thin stick; picking it up he pressed it down into the mud filled gun, stabbing at the mud, breaking it up, pulling it out from the gun. His hands shook, his body reacting to the cold.

He needed warmth and food. But these guns where his life line. He cleaned the gun. It took over an hour, but the guns were clean. Slamming the magazine back into the Beretta, he pulled back the slide can and pulled the trigger.

The bullet shot into the air with a satisfying bang. He smiled. The AK was fine, as were the other guns.

'Thank God,' he said as his body shook from the cold. Now his body needed work.

Chambers undid the knots on his pants, pulling them back on; they were like the rest of him, soaking wet. He looked down at his feet, bootless, one sock gone too. He looked up towards the path.

The woodlands that he had to hike were covered with rocks, stones and fallen bracken from the trees. His feet would get ripped apart. He took of his jacket. His hand went to his belt where the knife had been and his fingers meet nothing, then he remembered he had dropped it after getting the last boot off.

He grabbed the left sleeve of his shirt, pulling down on it hard. He ripped the sleeve off.

Sitting down on the muddy floor, he wrapped his sockless foot over and over as many times as he could, his toes sticking out the end of the once shirt sleeve. It was a poor protection but better than nothing. He did the same with the other foot with the other shirt sleeve. He looked down at his feet both wrapped in shirt sleeves, make do homemade shoes.

He looked at his compass; he had to head south-west if he was going to re-join the track to the miners' path.

He started to walk into the woods, every part of him soaking wet, his leg burning from being bashed around in the river. The AK was no longer on his back but in his hands.

He wondered if he could make it on foot with no boots. And back again. Could he ride the bike bare foot? Fuck, how the hell was he going to get over that river with the kid? All these thoughts and more went thought his mind. He walked on.

Chapter Four

His feet screamed with pain. Blood oozed out from the balls of his feet. The pain had made him grow pale. He wandered this way and that on the path, like a drunken fool. Already he had thrown up from the pain, his throat stung from it, the taste in his mouth was horrible.

He moved towards a great tree, resting on the trunk for a few seconds, his face burning with pain. He looked at his foot, a bloody pulp of matter attached to an ankle.

The sleeve of his shirt was no good. Already it was covered with dirt, ripped; it was starting to smell bad too, and the skin on his feet was ripped open, blood oozing out from them.

Small stones had dug into his feet. He kicked out, shaking his feet watching mud and dirt fall from them.

He looked down at his waterproof watch; it had been over thirty hours. And at his rate he doubted he could go on for much longer, let alone in the timeframe he and Brigance had agreed too and Hanna wouldn't give him an inch.

He walked on, gritting his teeth, fighting the pain. Hopefully, the pain would overpower him soon, it would hurt so much that it would stop hurting all together.

He walked on, after three steps his feet went from on fire to colder than to ice.

His foot then stopped working.

His foot fell from under him. He went down, dropping to one knee, pain flooring him.

He stabbed the butt of the AK into the ground, using it as a walking stick for a second, then with great effect he pushed himself forward.

I must go on, he thought, his mind racing, trying everything he could do to just move on. He walked on, staying close to the path but not on it, staying parallel to it, about two hundred and fifty yards within the treeline. Every now and then he moved back, making sure he could the light clay coloured path. It was long, thin, overgrown; littered with rocks and bits of trees, a few dead animals on the track. He then slipped back into the cool of trees.

He felt at home in the woods. As he marched on his painful feet, they sent stabbing sensations to his brain.

His body shook from stabs of pain that smashed down hard into his brain. But luckily it happened less and less. And for now he could still move.

He pushed on, walking harder and harder, when he saw it: the old miners' house. Chambers had forgotten about that.

He saw the top of the roof, broken on one half, the left side sinking in. Old rusty looking dark brown bricks. Only the skeleton of the building really remined.

He needed to check it out. There was a good chance there could be something in there. Boots? Maybe, hopefully.

He needed something, anything over his feet. The house was his best hope. He knew his feet couldn't take much more; It was only a matter of time before his feet gave in and then he was done.

He pushed on wondering if *they* would be in the house: the kidnapers.

It would be a good place to hide. But he doubted it. There was somewhere better, about ten miles up the road, in a deep rocky valley; a great place to see anyone coming.

And anyone after the kidnappers would have to go though it unless they wanted to climb for about nine hours up a hard cliff face.

He'd go to the miners' house. He had to check it out. It was around six p.m. As he moved towards the small, rusty building, he stood in the trees, watching, the AK-47 in his hands. He had smelled it, weed, and burning; someone or some people were in that building.

Chambers moved down low on a large oak tree, kneeling in its shade, the great shadow blocking him from view of the house.

He raised the AK-47's scope to his face. Looking down the scope of the rile, he checked out the house.

The windows were covered with thick, red, rusty metal slats; the slats were covered in holes, small, but he could see though them and they out of them. They blocked much of what was going on. But Chambers could see dark shadowy figures moving in the house.

He watched them though the scope of the gun.

They were drinking a lot from a bottle being handed around from face to face. He knew the smell of weed was way too strong for just for one person; two, three guys in there, easy.

He moved the scope down to the side of the building. He saw a collection of empty crushed beer cans, a lot of them.

He moved the rifle around the building. Was this the kidnapers? He took his head away from the scope looking at the building. If it was them they were way dumber then he had thought. Way dumber? If it was them, they knew nothing, nothing. Then why come here, to this terrible place, this mountain and how? They must have driven up the other path, must have taken them two days of driving and hiking.

He dropped down low, moving fast towards the right side of the building. He shot out from the tree line and in few short sharp steps he was next to the building, hiding under a small window. He waited, the AK-47 at his waist, hanging loose but in a tight iron grip, in his strong hands.

He stood under the window, listening. Music, loud angry, nasty, music, came out from under the windows. Racist music. Skinhead music, Nazi music.

Brigance had said it was a bunch of brothers that had been into the shop, not a bunch asshole Nazis.

He hated Nazis with the fire of a million suns, as most saw him as was one. His blood ran to his face, teeth bared.

Everyone saw him as a Nazi. Day in and day out, their sign, the sign of the Nazis sprayed on his house, the sign cut into *his* front door.

And there was them, the *Nazis*! How many times they tried to make him join, even swearing a blood vendetta on him when he told them to go *fuck* themselves.

He was an outcast from the normal people and from the racists; he was a man who lived nowhere.

Wanted by no one, trusted by no one. He was no one.

He moved to the door, body low, sweat pouring down from his face. A fast hand came up, wiping away the water from it. He could feel the salty sweat on his face. He stood next to the front door, his blood up, every inch of him wanting a fight.

His finger clicked the safety off. He was ready. He jumped at the door, slamming his shoulder into it. The door flew open with rusty crash.

He stood in the doorframe pulling the gun up. Looking inside the one room building, he saw them, wanting with all his might to pull that trigger. He raised the gun, pointing it at them. Three kids, teenagers no older then sixteen, ran back away from him, slamming into the rear wall. Half-drunk cans of the cheapest beer fell from their hands, landing hard on the floor, the amber liquid pouring out onto the floor, beer mixing with dirt.

The three Nazi-wanna-bes looked at Chambers. Eyes wide with shock, one moved towards a knife on the table.

Chambers saw the movement.

Chambers aimed the gun at them, pushing the rifle forward towards them, telling them without words to stay the fuck back.

Chambers' eyes burnt into them; one still had a beer can in his hands and he wanted him to drop it. Chambers voice came out as one loud commanding bark.

'Drop it!'

The kid threw his arms high into the air and fast in shock. The kid lost his balance, falling forward, arms and legs spinning, crashing into the old metal table in front of him. Chambers pointed the gun at the others. The Nazi kids look terrified.

Chambers returned the AK-47 to the kid who smashed into the table. He was small, head shaven, wearing a white T shirt, a black hand painted Swastika in the middle, a pair of light blue jeans and black army boots.

The others were dressed the same but darker, black jeans, brown boots, black T shirts with red Swastikas, made to look like dripping blood.

Chambers' eyes were transfixed by the Swastikas. He wanted... needed to pull the trigger on his gun. To kill them! To kill any man or women who wore that sign. You had no right or reason to live as far Chambers was concerned if you wore that sign.

'*Go to the back of the fucking wall!*' Chambers raged aloud, spit flying from his mouth.

The kids moved back but had nowhere to go. There heels crashed into the wall behind them.

The one in the white shirt fell over his own feet, trying to move away from Chambers. Crashing down hard onto the floor, he looked up at him. Chambers pushed the gun towards him.

'*Up!*' he bellowed.

The kid moved on his hands and knees, moving backwards like a spider. He hit the wall on his knees, looking up at Chambers. Chambers looked down at him, at them, at the Nazi kids and their sign.

A pounding rage welled up inside of him, his face a mask of pure rage. He hated this kid. The music was screaming and he looked towards it, the rage pumping inside his vines, as the hateful music kept on screaming.

"White Power, White Power, White Power!" the music screamed out, as if it was an old-fashioned vinyl record with a stuck needle.

Those words seemed to be played over and over, banging inside Chambers' very skull. The words seemed cut into his mind.

The pressure from the last two days was overpowering him.

He looked at the music player. He looked at the Nazi kids, hands up, standing waiting.

The rage was inside Chambers, looking for any chance to break out of him. He looked from them to the music.

'Just take it,' started one of them, pointing at the tiny pile of weed.

Chambers jibed the AK-47 at them; they jumped back from him.

Chamber turned, spinning on the spot, his eyes burning with rage. He pointed the AK at the music player, letting out a blaze of gunfire.

The player exploded in a ball of flames as the large bullets from the gun hit it.

The words "White Power" were cut off in the boom from the bullets.

'Where's the kid?' barked out Chambers.

The three looked shocked by this, as if they had no idea what he was talking about. The three looked from one and other then back to Chambers.

'Wh… what… what kid?' whispered one of them.

'The *kid*,' shot out Chambers. 'Where is *he*?'

'What kid, there is no kid,' someone said.

'Where is he?' screamed out Chambers.

The Nazi kids, shocked, shook their heads, fear screaming inside them. This guy with the AK was crazy, what was he talking about? *Kid*, what fucking kid?

'Please listen, there is no *kid*,' said one of them.

'The kid, George Rule. A black kid was kidnaped. Where is he?'

The two Nazis looked at each other. No idea what the hell he was talking about.

'A nigger?' said the one in the white shirt, still on his hands and knees on the floor.

Rage again flamed up inside Chambers' mind. He looked down at the kid.

'*Up!*' he said.

The kid stood, his hands high in the air.

'Walk towards me,' said Chambers.

The kid wanted to look to his friends. But he didn't, he did what he was told. He walked towards Chambers. When he was a few feet from him, Chambers swung the rifle, twisting, rotating his hips, smacking the butt of the AK-47 into the kid's face. The butt of the gun ripped out his mouth. Blood and three teeth went flying. The kid was knocked out before he hit the ground.

Then one of the other kids pissed himself, a large dark stain forming at the front of his pants, as they looked on in shock as the kid smashed to the ground. Chambers flicked the gun, blood spraying onto the floor.

Chambers walked towards the kid, itching to pull down hard on the trigger. But he was a kid, sixteen years old. He wanted to kill him, fire the gun right in the middle of that Nazi sign.

The kid didn't answer; he looked down at his friends, then to the floor, blood pumping out of his cut mouth and feeling the blood pooling inside his mouth. He was breathing in heavily, looking at the barrel of the Ak-47.

God, he could see down the end of the gun. He wanted to scream.

'How old I asked!' screamed Chambers again.

The kid shook from head to toe. He answered as best he could. 'Six… sixteen.' He just about got it out.

Chambers held the gun at him, wanting with all his heart to pull the trigger. But why?

This pissant kid knew nothing about Nazis.

If he actually saw pictures of Auschwitz he'd rip that shit off his chest. He knew nothing about the real world, and yet after the shit he had been though in the last thirty odd hours he wanted someone to pay.

Chambers' breath came in deep harsh lungsful of air, hoping the cool air would easy the rage inside of him. It didn't.

The kid looked at the man before him, his finger on the trigger, the barrel down on him. He didn't know what to do.

'Please, man, I'm not even into this Nazi shit.' He pulled at the T shirt, pulling at the Swastika on his chest. 'I just want to belong! Hell, since I was a kid they, teachers screamed at me because I'm white.' He pulled the shirt again. 'So I thought why not be one of them… but I don't believe.'

'So you support people who killed at least six million so you can fit in… is that what you're telling me?' Chambers screamed like a drill instructor.

The kid went down to his knees, hands up. This was the last change as far as he was concerned. On his knees, he raised his hands. 'Please, man, I'm begging you, don't kill me… I'm only sixteen!'

'So were some Nazis. Get up… *now*!'

The kid did so slowly, standing with hands high in the air.

Chambers lowered the gun.

'You're lucky, kid. If you were eighteen I'd kill you.'

With that and without thinking he lowered the gun and pulled the trigger.

The bullet shot out smashing into the boy's kneecap; it was blown apart, turning it into a bloody pulp. The kid's leg just hung on; the blood seemed to instantly vanish from his face. He stood for a second before falling into a pile on the ground.

Chambers spat at the kid, and then he heard something from outside. He turned as the door opened. A man stood in the doorway; he looked tall. The two saw each other just for a flash of a second. The man in the door had something in his hands.

Gun! thought Chambers, dropping to his knee without thinking, acting on training. The man in the door way was pulling something from his back. But when he saw the AK in Chambers' hands he threw up his hands, reaching out towards him, trying to scream out.

Chambers' lower jaw jammed down hard; he aimed the gun, the rage inside of him about to explode.

He saw the kid's sign of don't shoot. But his blood was up, the rage pounding in his body and mind. With a scream that never left his mind. Chambers pulled down on the trigger. There was an explosion from the end of the gun, a great flash of orange light came out of the rifle.

He fired out three quick bullets that slammed into his chest. The force of the bullets took him off his feet. He fell back, smashing down hard onto the woodland floor. With a small boyish scream of pure pain, he died, blood clouding into the air.

Chambers watched as blood came from the body, splintering around the walls and floor of the building.

Chambers stood, shock flying though his veins.

He stood slowly looking at the blood covering the doorframe, his eyes transfixed by it, not wanting to look down at the dead body. He forced himself to. Shock crashed into him. It was a kid, fourteen years old max, his chest covered with bullet holes, blood still pumping from his wounds, eyes open just staring at nothing, lost deep in pain and terror.

My eyes must look like that right now, thought Chambers.

The kid was white, shaved head. His once white T shirt was now blooming with blood, the Nazi sign still visible, under the blood and bullet holes. His shirt was burnt by the force of the hot bullets as they hit him. His skin was also cut open revealing muscle, tissue and bone.

Chambers stood over him looking at his small and skinny arms; they had marks on them. Not marks but tattoos. He lowered himself down, looking at them. No, again he was wrong not tattoos. But pen marks, he marked himself with the Nazi's sign in pen.

'Fuck,' he said, 'he was only fourteen, if that.'

He looked at his body. Looking at his hands, he saw it by his left knee. He must have dropped it when he was shot. He took the gun, pressing the button on the handle, catching the magazine as it fell. Looking in to the magazine, his mouth went dry; he replaced the magazine back into the BB gun, the black plastic BB gun; he held it tight, resting the gun on his forehead.

'These fucking kids,' he whispered then threw the gun as far and hard as his strong right arm could.

He heard it fall softly into the bushes. He moved, trying to force himself not to look at the dead kid on the ground, as the dead kid's right arm twitched.

Chambers re-entered the building. He looked down at the other Nazis, one passed out though pain; he would never walk properly again. But he'd live. And he hated himself.

The last three were against the wall, looking down at one friend dead, the other in a heap blood pumping from the wreck of his leg, then he passed out, as he looked at Chambers. All the Nazis were dealt with one way or the other.

He looked down at his feet. His one sock once bright and white now a grey and black, cut up with mud and blood.

He looked at the four kids in the building.

Luckily the one with broken teeth was tall and had big feet. He dropped to his knee, undoing his large shiny black boots, pulling them of, slipping them on his own injured feet.

It took whole minutes to get the damn things on. His feet screamed out in pain as he pulled the heavy leather boots on his fucked-up feet.

The two kids just watched deep in shock, not knowing if he would kill them next.

After lacing up the boots, he stood as best he could. He moved in the boots, they were tight and hurt him. But they were a lot, lot better than his bare feet.

The tops of the boots were tight too. He was on his haunches bouncing up and down on the boots trying to loosen them.

He looked to the wall at his side, looking at the great white Swastika painted on to the wall, he looked at as it loomed over him.

How could he have looked at thing that *they* had put up having no idea what it meant? They had put it up, and yet... yet as he looked at that sign of hate and evil, he felt like he was worse than them.

He turned back to the others still standing, the other kid on the floor passed out trying to breath. He had made up his mind.

'Turn around, face the wall!' Chambers screamed. They did, their faces close to the rotting old brick. They were going to die, they knew it.

Chambers aimed the AK-47 at their backs about to pull the trigger, when he ran as best he could out of the house towards the tree line.

One kid dead, his body cooling in the summer air. Already bugs had started to land on his body. They were also landing on the kid with busted leg. The others just stood there on the wall, one friend dead, the other would never walk right again. He had got off lightly. He killed himself two weeks later. The other two never spoke of that day ever again.

Chapter Five

Hanna, even for a millennial, was pissed off. Twenty-four hours had passed, over twenty-four hours had passed, in fact. And there was no sign of that son of a bitch.

He had taken her money and ran. Never trust a white man, er mother had told her. Her father had told her too. Hell, she had been told her brother. And now she had trusted a whitey and where had it got her and her brother? Lost in the pine.

Her eyes were on the tall trees that moved softly in the wind, their branches gently rocking, whipping back and forth almost hypnotically.

She was standing on the wooden porch, the cold wind moving around her as she rocked on the balls of her of feet.

Her eyes were watery, filled with dark tears desperate to fall from her eyes, as she looked at the trees moving over and over. Her little brother was lost out there. And her just a dumb girl standing around while the man did the work. The white man too.

She stepped from the porch, sitting on its edge, wondering, hoping by some miracle that he was alive. She had read stories, tales about the deaths of loved ones. That their families could feel it in their hearts or souls. Feel the moment of their death.

At that thought the tears did come. A lot of wet yet silent still tears, fell from her eyes. From behind her she felt the footfalls from the race traitor, Brigance.

He stood behind her, looking out across the wide-open trees standing like soldiers on guard… waiting. He was their gatekeeper stopping the darkness that was there, holding it back, the darkness from the normal world.

Brigance looked out then across the plain, his eyes zooming in on the tall trees, then they fell to his watch. Time was burning away, the time for him to make a heavy decision.

Brigance didn't trust the girl and she didn't trust him. He looked up at the grey sky; the black clouds were moving in over the cabin. He looked down at the girl, her tears pouring from her eyes, body shaking with powerful silent sobs.

Hanna's fingers went inside her pocket, touching the small white cellphone she had found in Brigance's drawer. He had a drawer full of burner cell phones. Soon she would call the police.

'Time is burning,' whispered Brigance.

Chambers walked on. The heat was powerful. He had already drunk too much water. He knew soon he would be out of water and if he was out, then that was a problem… he could die in this heat without water. Just another thing on this mountain that could kill you.

His clothes stuck to him. He moved his body at odd angles, trying to get the sticking clothes off his skin. As he moved his clothes stuck harder to him. He pulled at them, trying to tear them from his slick wet skin.

The mosquitos had come too, great dark clouds that came over him. He brushed them aside as best he could.

He walked through the woods looking down at the path. He smiled to himself; the path was there, but it had changed colour, it was no longer light brown but a dirty, dusty grey.

Good, he thought, *it was about time too.*

The path was turning grey, that meant he was getting closer to the slate cliffs. That was a tell-tale sign, that he was getting close to the valley, only the valley had that shade of grey rocks on this side of the mountain.

He pressed on, his feet burning, his breaths coming in large and deep, yet his lungs felt empty.

He moved towards the cliffs when it happened. His legs went. He crashed faced down on the hard, rocky, nasty ground.

Small rocks cut into his face. His mind was burning with more than just heat or shock or pain. He was angry, he felt it, starting to break mind.

His fingers dug into the soil of the Earth, his hands turning into balls of rage. He pulled himself forward, feet digging into the dirt and rocks as he pushed himself forward, when he lost his footing and his body crashed.

His mind was screaming to keep on fighting, to keep moving forward, this was goal, his mission, his passion, his destiny. He would find this kid, dead or alive. He threw. himself forward, into the heat of the sun, as its rays burnt down on him.

Hours passed, the sun moved slowly, turned across the mountains, making deep cool shadows that he moved through.

The sun started to set. Chambers stopped, falling hard against the trunk of a tree, his body aching, muscles burning.

He looked up at the sun, watching it slide down below the mountain side. Another day lost; night had again set on Steel Mountain and he was behind schedule. Time was burning away.

He started walking on, his feet burning, moving as best he could, the dark blue of night tuning into a deep black. But tonight there were no clouds so moonlight would be available. He moved on through the bush and hard stones of the mountain.

In the sliver moonlight, he saw it, the slate cliffs standing tall, d in the moonlight. A great stone valley. A gateway, a gateway to his redemption, but it looked like the mouth of hell to Chambers.

Chapter Six

Hanna was done. Brigance stood before her in the cabin as the long shadows of the night started to form. She was done. The time given was almost over, and Hanna had enough.

She had had it with this. Now she knew, she had made a mistake. She should have never trusted a white man as in ever. She still didn't understand why Brigance was protecting Chambers. Hanna was so angry with Brigance; he was there standing in front of her protecting this white asshole. Why?

'Call the police!' she bellowed, her dark face flashing with hate, rage.

Brigance had spent the last few hours fighting non-stop with this brat. Brigance was getting tired of it. He had zero intentions of calling the police on Chambers.

He had to buy Chambers more time. This racist brat was going to ruin the whole thing. The cops had no money because of snowflakes like this one and her parents and teachers, hell, everyone. Screaming that the police where racist but *they* needed them, they called the cops first and when they couldn't help, they screamed racist even lounder.

They had done it defund the police and watched crime skyrocket from their rich ivory towers.

'*Now!*' screamed Hanna, her voice cutting though Brigance's mind.

Brigance was done. His eyes locked on hers, rage building up inside of him now. He walked fast across the cabin without thinking. His right hand flew up to his shoulder then down hard and fast, his flat palm slamming down across her face.

Hanna fell back, losing her footing, crashing down onto the rough wooden floor of the cabin.

Brigance's eyes widened with shock at what he had done. He had slapped a little girl.

The kid moved backwards in shock, moving on her hands and knees like a spider, her dark eyes looking up in shock at Brigance. New terror started to move inside her mind.

She was in danger, so was her brother; she needed help just as much as he did. Her hand moved to her pocket, pulling out the cellphone she had stolen from Brigance's cabin, her fingers moving over the screen, her fingers working overtime about to call the 911, when Brigance, moving fast brought down a large and powerful brown leather boot, down on the phone and her hand. He crushed both, the cellphone and her hand, under his boot.

Hanna let out a shout of pain as Brigance twisted his heavy boot fast from right to left, breaking the phone completely

Hanna let out a scream, pulling her hand out from under his boot. She looked at her hand, the skin was broken, long thin rivers of red blood poured from her hand.

She looked down at the cell, broken, and useless. She looked up at Brigance as he dropped his foot down hard again on to the phone again, watching as his heavy booted foot crashed her life line into nothing.

She wanted to hurt him with all her strength. To cut him, to shoot him, kill him.

She saw it, the door it was open, that was her last hope. She jumped for it.

Brigance saw her, throwing his arm out at her. Hanna dropped down under it as Brigance's arm swung around her, missing her head by inches.

Hanna bolted for the door, hearing the heavy booted feet storming towards her.

She got to the door flying out into the store. She jumped over the counter, crashing down on the floor. She moved fast on her aching feet, knees screaming, but still she was flying towards the open door of the store.

She fell out over the porch of the cabin, crashing into the hard grass. Getting to her feet, she ran then lost her footing in her mad dash to escape. She fell, falling down the grassy mountain side.

Brigance moved out of the store, seeing Hanna running fast down the hill.

Chambers sit down on a log, his feet up and boots off, watching the ridge of the two valleys, wondering if there was anyone up there. He smiled to himself. *They would-be first-class fools if they didn't. Have a look out.*

He sat using the treeline as cover. If there was someone up there with a pair of binoculars or even a rifle scope, they would be hard pushed to see him. But he could see the ridge very well. It did seem empty; there was little to no movement. He sat for a long time watching the long shadows, that had been deepening for hours. Soon it would be full darkness. And when that fell he would move.

He looked at his feet. There was a bad smell coming from them. The skin looked weird, puckering up, from walking with injured, wet feet. Also around the edges of his feet had large red ugly marks.

He reached forward, gently touching the red marks on his foot; a flaring of pain shot though his body.

Not good, he thought, through gritted teeth.

He wondered how long he could go with his feet like this. The pain was bad and when he put the boots back on he wondered if he could even walk on them.

Pain, white hot pain, had screamed in his mind, making him bite down hard on his teeth, as his sore skin touched the tough, hard leather of the boots. Somehow he got them on and laced up.

He looked though the AK-47 scope. Looking at the high ridge line above him, looking for something… anything: a figure standing, thin rays of blue grey smoke from a cigarette, movement of someone or something, just something. He spent over an hour watching all parts of the two ridge lines until he was sure there was no one there.

It can't be, he thought, looking from the scope, using his bare eyes, then replacing his eye to the scope, looking at the ridge line, shaking his head.

He was sure that the ridge was empty. Every time he was about to go, that voice would come back to him. There had to be a watcher, any fool would have a man, at least one man up there.

He waited, the scope to his eye, just watching, thinking. There had to be someone up there.

After another hour of watching it came to him that there was no one up there.

He walked on deep in thought. It made no sense. These people had no idea what they were doing.

That made his pace quicken. These fools didn't know what they were doing and that made them very dangerous.

They would panic and fight. And panicked man with few choices, tired and scared, would fight hard, that would be a tough fight. Made worse if the kid was alive.

Chambers walked through the night, using a small flash light on his AK-47, shining it from time to time on the woodland floor, not daring to use the light for any long periods of time, for fear of it giving him away.

He moved for hours in the woods, his feet hitting into the fallen trees, leaves and sticks that littered the forest floor.

He came across a huge oak, that had been brought down by lightning. It was propped up about three feet from the floor.

Dropping to his belly he crawled under the great oak, hoping he wouldn't knock it, hoping it wouldn't fall on him.

His feet were burning and throbbing with pain. He was hoping the pain would ease soon, he didn't want to take any pills as he needed his mind as clear as he could; pain plus pills could make a problem for him, very much so in a fight.

He wanted to listen to his body to just sit, to sleep. To have a different pair of socks and boots to wear. But he didn't; he just had to keep moving around the mountain forest, thinking with every strange sound that it could be a bear or wolf. Or someone like him, a killer, waiting in the darkness. He tried to keep his mind in check, but almost every sign had to be looked into, as he moved closer to the rocky valley.

Then, after a four-hour hike through the valley, with feet burning, legs screaming as he pushed up the mountain, stopping to rest on tree after tree, his lungs burning, body aching all the way, he reached one of the clearings on the mountain. His eyes looked up; he was high up on the mountain and yet, the summit of the valley was still high under the moonlight.

These guys had picked the perfect place to hide, they some smarts; but then they might not be there at all for all he knew. God, what if no one was there. They had to be, they had to be. Or it was over.

He made up the valley looking down at the woods below. He made it down walking slowly and easily down the valley. There was good moonlight as he marched down to the bottom within an hour and a half and straight back to yet another wood, but he was close to the cabin or hut.

He had seen it before years ago, the last time had come this way in fact.

He never went this deep into the mountain if he could help it. The last time he had he had been in one hell of a fight, got a bullet for his trouble, and he was likely to get another one tonight too. The fight would be tonight.

He tried not to think about it as he hiked and hiked through the trees; he must have passed tree after tree after tree. Then he smelt it, smoke. He tasted it to. He slowed, his body lowering, as he saw what looked like a clearing in the woods. Fast, he dropped down low, zooming to one of the larger trees, the AK-47 was brought up a little; he was readying himself for the fight that always seemed ready to come at any second.

He looked through the scope of his gun and saw only a pile of rocks with black smoke coming from the top, like smoke from gunshot. It was the chimney of the hut. Someone was in there. A fight was about to happen. Chambers cocked the gun.

He eased forward to the treeline opening when he saw it, a small stone and log hunt.

Chambers stopped watching, moving slowly, hiding from sight.

Chambers moved the AK-47 to under his armpit, watching the cabin though his scope, looking at the dark cabin bathed in shadows.

This had to be it. This was the only place where they could take him, there was nowhere else for miles and miles, just an old unused mine, way too dangerous to hide in.

He wanted to open up with the AK to fire down at that the cabin. To just pull the trigger until the gun was empty, to kill everything inside no matter who it was. His thumb moved to the safety catch, snapping it to the off position, then his finger curled around the trigger.

Chapter Seven

God I want a cigarette! thought Chambers as he kneeled, his eyes glued on the hut. He needed a cigarette, he ached for one. But he also knew that even if he did have one with him, it would be one of the dumbest things to do.

God, my legs. He stood, resting the left side of his body on the large tree, feeling the blood move around his body, easing the pain from one limb but then another limb or body part would call out in pain as one part of his body was rested at the cost of another body part, all of this while staying within the great shadows of the trees. Staying in the camouflage of the deep dark shadows.

His eyes, mind and all his senses were transfixed on the cabin, looking for any clue that there could be something wrong with the hut. He looked for any sign of movement. Something, anything. Then it happened. He saw... something. Movement.

His body went tight; he stopped his body fidgeting dead. He lowered down, lowered into an attack position, eyes raking the cabin.

He saw nothing, heard nothing, had he just imaged the movement? Maybe it was his body and mind being tired, making him want to just get it over and done? Maybe... just maybe.

He sniffed the air, opened his mouth, letting his tongue out to taste the air. All of him was looking, feeling for any sign that things there not as they should be.

Nothing. All was well, or at least seemed the same as before, but he didn't think so or feel so. A feeling, a bad shadow had crossed his mind and soul.

He dropped down on to his side, pressing himself to the trunk of the large tree. In a flash the AK-47 was in his hands, safety off, scope to his eye, the rifle being moved over the cabin.

Looking at the cabin, he wondered what to do. He had to get a closer look at the wood and stone building.

Hell, the kid, could be in there. He had to know.

Moving fast and low on his belly, he made it across the path from the treeline, looking more like some sick prehistoric snake, then a man.

His fingers touched the weather-beaten wood of the hut's panels. He stood an inch or two from the cabin, making sure that his powerful frame didn't hit the wood of the building, making sure not to give away his position. He was under the window; he was sure as he could be that he was unseen.

Chambers was low, right under a window. He looked up from the window frame, his head under it, easing up from under the windowsill.

Chambers' head popped to the side of the window frame, looking in though the small and only window on this side.

He breathed out, seeing his breath mist up in the window pane, a clear give away of his position. His hand shot out, quickly yet gently rubbing the pane, taking away the mist from his breath. The window made the smallest of sounds.

He dropped down low as he thought he saw movement, his body pressed on the wood, as he tried to stay small and out of sight.

Keeping low, he eased back from the window. After a while, he relooked in, holding in his breath in his lung as long as he could, then letting it out in a silent gasp of air, pushing the air over his bottom lip, so as not to mist the pane again.

His vision glued on the window, he eased forward, looking though the pane, eyes rolling from the window to the place where he thought the door would be. He looked in, his head bobbing up and down fast, catching glimpses of the inside.

Chambers saw little, trying to make sure he was not seen by those within. He was starting to wonder if there was even anyone in the damn thing.

Maybe they had a fire waiting for them when they returned. Maybe they had run. Maybe… maybe they had never been here.

Maybe, maybe… And fucking… maybe!

His temper was starting to flare up. Without knowing, one of his hands twisted to a ball and he knocked on the hard-rough wood of the cabin.

He froze. He not meant to do it, but he had. He had to do something. But not that. That was wild, that was crazy.

The clock was ticking; he was on his own; he trusted Hanna as much as she did him.

He trusted Brigance with his life, as Brigance did with him. But Brigance had his limits; that kid Hanna would be a lot of trouble.

If she called the police, the police would use him as a reason to go crazy. Could that have been the real reason why she hired him? Use him to get the wheels of a defunded judge going? No, she hated cops more than him. To Hanna and her family blue skin was the worst skin.

If they had a suspect (him) then they could push the panic button. The defunding would be over.

A little black kid taken by a white man and not just a white man: an ex-cop, ex-army and a nigger killer.

Chambers closed his eyes, lowering his head, when he heard it, a sound as clear as day. A door… a door had opened. Someone was there.

Shit, he thought. He been lost in his thoughts, forgetting he had knocked on the wood.

Shit, his face said without words, as he looked towards the sound. He had to get his shit together.

He was out in the open, no cover. No nothing. He rushed as fast as he could, back into the welcoming gloom and dark shadows of the black forest. Within a second he was lost, invisible in the sweet and welcoming gloom, his body just a shadow under the tree's great shadow.

He looked on, watching, his breaths coming fast and shallow, as he kneeled, waiting... Nothing happened, no movement. But the sound of the opening door echoed in his mind.

He tracked with his rifle from one end of the hut to the other, waited for a second or two then he tracked back to the other end of the hut, waiting, watching. Nothing. He turned his head away from the gun and looking down towards the cabin, watching it again with his own naked eyes.

The hut was still just the slowly moving grey smoke moving up and up and up.

What was this person playing at, he thought.

Chambers shook his head, thinking that he was losing it. He wanted to find that kid no matter what, dead or alive, but his heart yearned to find the boy alive. He did want to find the kid alive. For the love God, he needed to.

His mind was overpowering him with all the memories; thoughts of years and years of repression came back to him. The years of hate, the shouting, the screaming people throwing shit in his face. The hands punching, clawing his face and oh God, the words thrown at him non-stop, for years and years he was called a racist, a monster, a nigger killer, over and over. To see the look on his father's face; to hear the attack on him and his mother; to see his father on national TV saying that he his son was a monster, that has own father said that on TV: his son was a racist and should be in prison for murder. He didn't murder that man. He killed him but he didn't murder him.

It was a lawful death; the hangman isn't a killer. But he was a poster boy for the crazy left. No, the crazy world.

Ex-army, ex-cop, a white, male, straight American. It wasn't hard for them to demonize him. This was his last hope, his only hope, to just be a person, to get something normal.

Something moved, a shadow like him, and his body and mind snaped too it.

A man walked from the edge of the cabin. Chambers watched the shadowy figure walked around the edge of wooden house, stopping at the place where only a few moments before, Chambers was standing. The man looked around the cabin. Finding nothing, he moved back inside. The door closed softly, the sound lost in a gust of wind.

A light came on in the little window. Chambers sat up on one knee, as pulled the AK-47's scope to his eye.

The gun was on that window as he watched the dim dull, amber light.

A candle light was it, he thought. No, too bright, an oil lamp? Maybe.

He watched on, looking though the scope. He had to make a choice; he couldn't stay here, just watching, he had to make a move. He knew someone was in that cabin. But his choices where slim.

He could call out to the people inside?

Great plan to get your head blown off, or the kid's.

He could creep up on the hut.

Dangerous. Very dangerous. And the last time all had manged to find out was there was someone inside.

184

He could just keep watching, wait for something or anything.

That could take hours, all night and all day.

His mind buzzed as he watched though the scope. He waited, his mind turning like waves in a storm. He had do something. There was little to no movement in the cabin, but he had to it.

They must know someone was there, they had heard his crazy knock. Had they told themselves it was the wind? Or some other bullshit? They had to be on edge.

He laid the AK down on the grass taking the Storm pistol from his belt. Dropping the magazine into his open hand, he checked it: bullets full. He gently pushed the magazine back into the gun, cocking it, sliding the slide back, hammer down; it was ready.

This too went on the grass next to the AK-47. Then the magnum 357 was take out. He opened the cylinder in the dim light of the night. He saw all six cylinders filled with powerful bullets, bullets that could take off limbs. He closed the cylinder, cocking the gun as quietly as he could, pulling it all the way back; thumb clicking the safety off. Then that two went down with the other guns.

He did the same with the subcompact, that too was full and ready. He laid it with the others. Only one gun to check. And he knew they were all full and ready.

He picked up the AK, doing the same thing, taking the magazine out of the rifle, checking it, seeing it was full. He'd known it was, but he had to check, it was an OCD thing he did before a fight.

He replaced the magazine back into the rifle and it clicked home softly; it was a soft sound but in the still woods that click seemed as loud as a gunshot.

His eyes went straight to that dark and still hut. The light inside flickered, as if someone was standing in front of it. He paused, watching, dropping the AK down on the woodland floor.

His hand went straight to the 357, eyes never moving from the cabin. His hand brought the gun up at the window of the cabin. His other hand went to his wrist, holding it tight and straight.

His eyes where transfixed on that window. He looked down the long barrel of the gun, staring at the small bright orange blaze of glow in the dark paint, on the end of the gun, helping him see and aim in the darkness.

The light in the window moved, flickering as the oil burnt in the lamp. Was that it, just the light from the oil lamp moving? He paused, holding the gun still. He held on to it, watching. Nothing happened.

He privately promised the cabin that things would happen and soon, very soon.

The 357 magnum went back to the floor. He had the AK in his hands, thumb moving to the gun's switches. Should he put the gun into one shot per-fire? More careful to have the gun that way. But if there were many of them, he would be at a disadvantage. The three shot at a time? Safer maybe, but once again if there was a lot of them. They would have guns. Lots of them, too, if they were smart. Then he would be at a disadvantage. No good in dying for this kid.

So should he go fully automatic? But there was a chance, a very good chance, that he would be hurt or that the boy would be killed.

He flicked the switch to a three shot. This would be the best, he thought. His eyes blazed like a vampire, readying himself for the fight.

His thumb moved to the safety switch, turning it off with a click.

He placed the gun back on the ground, taking the Storm from the grass to replace the gun on his belt. He took the 357-magnum, sliding it back into the shoulder holster. He was about to take the AK-47 when he took his extra bullets out, opening the box and emptying them into his pocket, the right pocket. The front left was for the 357 bullets. The Beretta's extra ammo was in clips.

It was then he picked up the AK-47, moving the rifle to his waist slowly.

It was time. He moved, cat-like, his eyes locked on the hut, keeping away from the window as best he could. The light was his enemy.

Moving around the biggest trees, he used them as cover. The shadows where his friends. He eased forward towards the cabin again.

The people who made this cabin were smart; they had cut down the closest trees, making a clearing, making it very hard to sneak up on.

He was at the edge of the trees. He hid behind the last tree on the left. Sliding down on his belly, he moved snake like to the hut, eyes raking every inch of it, looking for any sign that he had been seen.

His eyes darted to the rough ground as he moved over it, checking for anything that could betray him to those in the hut, moving carefully over dry sticks and leaves.

He made it to the cabin. Standing slowly, he rested his body on the hard wood at the very edge of the cabin. He eased his back on the wood, turning his head to the cabin, his ear resting on the wood listening hard for any sound inside. He closed his eyes tight, listening with all his might. He could hear little…

Was that a footstep, he wondered, gripping the AK-47 tighter in his hands, his knuckles going bright white.

He pushed himself hard to the warm, moss-covered wood. The AK rested across his chest. He listened hard for any sound coming from within the cabin or for any movement going on inside.

He listened hard, hearing nothing.

He moved to his haunches in one fast motion, keeping low trying not to smash his body into the wood of the cabin, not wanting to let them know he was there.

He waited again, his body tight, muscles stiff and unmoving, waiting, his ears wide open, listening for anything that could help him. There was nothing. He moved up towards the window pressing himself to the edge of it, listening deeply.

He eased his head towards the window, looking in, one quick look. He saw nothing, just like last time, but he knew why. He was moving too fast. He'd have to take a longer look. He eased himself around, looking in looking for longer this time.

He saw three men sitting around an old beaten table.

He looked hard and took in a lot. Two were eating. The other was in a chair reading.

Chambers dropped down low, waiting, not wanting to risk looking for too long.

He waited for as long as he thought he needed.

Now, check now!

With that, he moved again, looking through the window. He was wrong: four not three.

He looked around the room, head at the edge of the window frame, looking as best as he could, eyes large, wide, as if blinking was an evil thing.

He looked more around the cabin. The cabin seemed to be just one room, but he couldn't see the boy.

He looked down at the opposite wall of the cabin. Behind the table where the two sat was a small narrow bed was there and… he moved, pushing his face closer to the glass… and… and yes!

A boy — black, beaten, around ten — was there on the bed, tied up, unmoving. He had found him.

His eyes went wide with shock. He let out a gasp with the shock.

One of the men at the table heard him, looking up. Chambers moved back fast, fast enough he hoped, his head and body zooming back into the gloom.

The man wouldn't see him, just the movement. He dropped down low, his face a red mask of rage. How could he be so fucking stupid? He had broken a golden rule. He had learnt nothing in the Middle Eastern wars. Never give your position away, ever.

The man in the cabin had heard it, the sound of his gasp. It was the sound they been waiting for, been on guard for.

Chambers heard chairs being pushed back, the sounds of bodies being thrown into action. Christ, they had heard his knock. This would be the last time, he was an old fool wanting to fight. Did he care about the boy? Or did he want to kill, let out the built-up hate that was in his heart? Then the sounds of rushing feet came towards him, no time for philosophy.

Chambers had to move fast, and he did, low down under the window, zooming to the other side of the cabin. He bolted as fast and as quietly as he could, past the clearing and into the shadows of the trees, body low, AK tight to his chest.

Chambers had ran hard, pushing himself past the treeline, making sure he couldn't be seen by anyone, but still he could see. Hell, he wasn't that far away, a good flashlight would find him, but he could still get good and clean shots off.

He was low, making the most of the shadows around him. Taking a quick glance he saw the shapes of four men, standing looking around at the tree line, the men standing looking into the tree line. Then after seeing nothing moving around the cabin, they looked for any sign of Chambers.

The cabin was empty.

Should I kill them now? he thought.

He moved the AK-47, ready to do so.

Then it hit him. What had he seen?

Could he fire on unarmed people, shoot them in the back? They seemed unarmed; he needed to look closer.

He twisted his body around the tree, making dammed sure he was hard to see. The AK-47 came up slowly. He looked down the scope.

Already they were starting to fan out looking for him. He heard their shouts and calls perfectly. Then he heard their guns being cocked. Sweat trickled from his skin as he turned the gun's scope. He had not seen them get their guns. He didn't like that.

He moved the scope to the window of the cabin trying to look in fast. The cabin was empty. He could only see the wooden floorboards and nothing else. Then he heard it, the gunshot. The shot boomed out.

These boys meant business. These boys were into something. Hell, this was Steel Mountain, no good men here.

He had to make a move. pen fire… no, he had to know. If they were not the right people, the gun fight could kill him and let the real kidnapers know he was here.

He had to know. And yet how? He couldn't just walk down and look... *The scope*, he thought.

He looked at it. It was big and a little heavy. That was a good sign though, as weight was a sign of a good build. The glass was good and very powerful. That would be the key, if he could just move to the right position.

He looked at the four, moving out to the edges of the clearing, trying to stay close to the cabin, using it as a lighthouse.

He had one choice, to stay in the tree line, use the trees and the dark. He eased down from the heavy oak tree's shadow, picking a medium sized pine as his next point to hide. He crawled down to it, his body moving over the dead and dry leaves.

Then... a light, bright and white, shot out, missing his leg by an inch.

He bit down hard into the inside of his mouth, stopping the scream of fright, that was fighting to escape his mouth. He rolled into the pine as the flash light went over the oak he had been hiding behind.

Shit! he thought. The last thing he needed was to be seen; in a flashlight beam he would be fucked.

He moved down low to the pine. He pressed his strong frame down into the dirt and dead leaves, looking.

The man with the flashlight was shining it high to his right.

He eased down the AK-47 up to his eye, thinking he would have to shoot this guy, kidnaper or not.

He rested on the bark of the tree, bringing the gun up to shoulder height.

His nostrils flared with quick deep intakes of air and up went the gun. If the flashlight went anywhere near the scope it would shine like a beacon.

Fuck, he thought. Even his thoughts were whispers, as if his enemy could hear his thoughts.

The light was shining away from him at the other side of the wood. Chambers had already seen the next tree to go for. He shot to it, moving deer like.

He made it to the tree, dropping to his knees, hiding. He popped his head out from behind the tree and looked down at the hut; he was at a good angle.

From his place he took fast looks though the scope; he thought he was at a good angle to see the bed from here.

He waited and watched, looking out from the tree's side, like a ghost in the woods.

The man with the light was still shining it over the trees, way to the right from where he was.

Good, he thought. *Keep shining it over there*. The light went out, he heard the click.

Chambers smiled. He had seen this before.

A man searching with a flash ight will do this from time to time. Turn it off. Wait a few moments, listening, then in a flash turn it back on, on an area they thought the enemy was.

Chambers smiled, waiting for it… then, *Shit*.

Chambers' face fell. The man had turned on his hips in a fast turn, switching on the light.

The light smashed onto a tree, the tree where he was hiding.

As the light hit the tree the light pooled on to him. He twisted his body fast behind the tree, rolling his shoulders in, knees up, head down.

He had dropped the rifle which fell into a small mound of dead leaves, blocked by the tree.

He kept his body tight. Had he seen him? *No*, otherwise bullets would be flying towards him.

But he obviously thought he had seen something, as the beam of light stayed where it was. He waited.

The man with the light waited. And waited. And waited. Chambers was left as naked and needy as a baby… then the light went out.

He dropped low, rolling out looking down towards them.

The men where in a ring talking softly, facing the treeline not far from him. The one who had fired the flash light at him must have moved away to the others.

Chambers looked for the AK-47, found it, grabbed it, feeling his manhood return to him. The scope went to his eye. He looked at the window and saw him, the boy who had haunted his mind, for what seemed like an age. He was there, he had the image of the boy from Hanna's photo burnt into his mind. He knew that face. It was him.

The boy's face was swollen, bloody and bruised, his lips dry and cracked. Blood and other fluids oozed form his face. His clothes where soiled, his hands covered in dried blood. His hands and legs were tied tight with thick old blood covered rope.

The ropes were heavy, thick, twisted viciously around and around his ankles, wrapped around and around until his feet and lower legs looked as if some great, dirty, brown snake had twisted around him, waiting for its chance to rip him, tear him, eat him, kill him.

Tears, hot and heavy, mixed with the layer of salty sweat that covered the boy's face.

The four kidnappers moved around the hut, staying close to the small pools of amber light that shone out though the two small ill-fitting windows.

Chambers had moved higher into the trees' ridgeline. Looking down at them, he was ready.

He slipped his shirt free from the waist band of his pants, using to wipe the sweat from his face, taking his time to cool his mind; to push away the sadness, fear and worry from it.

It was time to go to work.

Turn the fear into rage, he thought. God, he wished that Hanna could see this.

He smiled to himself cruelly.

The people who kidnapped her brother where not the Klan, not Nazis or other evil white people. They were Black!.

That would have broken Hanna, he thought, to see that, to see the end of the bullshit, she had been fed from birth.

Evil has no colour or race. Evil is evil.

To see what they had done to her brother…

Hell, she was young, she would learn. The world isn't black and white, good and evil. Evil people can do good, and good people have done some of the worst things in the world, in the name of goodness.

Chambers knew, he knew that skin colours meant nothing, race nothing, gender… nothing. It's hearts and minds. Good people come in all shapes, races, and sexes. All in between, so why would evil be any different.

Chambers' fingers went to the two back up guns making sure the holsters where unbuckled.

Chambers, was ready. His face darkened, went dead, lost in thoughts of murder and death.

It looked as if he was mediating. He was ready. He knew what do and how to do it.

He took a knee (to kill better) and was ready to do the thing, maybe the only thing he was ever good at: killing.

The AK-47's butt went to his armpit, locked and loaded, safety off. *At last*, he thought, *I am complete*.

Chapter Eight

Hanna had never been so afraid for herself in her whole life. She was running without thought, running without direction. She fled as fast as she could, crashing through the thick, long grass.

She was trying to get down the mountain. Her feet slammed down on the grass. She slipped over, falling backwards on the grass, sliding down fast, dirt falling up around her, arms pumping as tried to get to her feet. She fell to her knees, sliding again. Jeans ripping, skin tearing, blood oozed down from the fresh rips on her flesh.

Grass and small stones went into the open wounds, stinging and burning her. Tears of fear and pain shot though her body. Her mind was on fire. She threw herself forward. She got to her feet, but the angle of the hill had her speed up, she was going to lose her feet. But she had to go, she was more jumping then running.

Her body hit the hard ground. She slid down the hill, falling over and over herself, seeing nothing but grass then the inky blue, black, star-filled sky. Her body slammed down, winding her.

Her body was twisting over itself. Fresh blood was running form her body as new wounds formed on her, skin slitting open.

She felt the blood flow down her body. The speed she was moving was shocking as she fell down the steep hill.

She tried to stop but every time she thought she had a good foothold, the force of her falling speed made her fall back, towards the grass. She kicked out her feet, jamming down hard onto the ground.

Her left foot went under her. Then her whole body weight smashed down on that foot.

She felt the snap of the bone breaking as she fell down.

Her scream was long and loud. Her head was spinning as she came to a stop. Her head resting on the grass she heard it: thundering footsteps. It was him, he was after her. She let out a moan.

What should I do? she thought. *Hide*, her mind fired at her.

But where? And with a broken foot. But she had to try. She stood; she screamed, hitting the ground hard, with the pain in her foot.

She had hoped it was only an impact pain. But she was wrong, deep she knew it.

She tried to stand again but her foot was too bad. She went down, bashing down hard. The pain zoomed though her body and mind, her eyes popping with pain.

She was done. Not because Chambers or even Brigance said it, but because she said it. She was done.

She had failed, she had failed her brother.

She had failed to find the right man to find him.

She had failed to make sure he did the job. She was at the worst place in the world, she needed help… she needed the police.

Those racist monsters in blue, who always killed blacks. Who made sure blacks didn't get to vote. Who pulled them over. Who threw blacks in prison for fun. And they were what she needed.

See what I'm brought too, she spat in her mind.

She heard his footsteps, fresh tears falling down her face.

She felt it, warm, strong yet soft hands touching her shoulder.

The hands gently turned her over. Brigance pulled her into his arms, walking back up the hill, carrying her up the hill back to his house.

Hanna looked up at the stars, seeing them overhead, spinning, turning, moving, billions of years old.

Brigance spoke soothingly to her. She didn't hear him. She was lost in her own mind, thinking of her brother, thinking of her family… all was lost.

This race traitor, Brigance, was protecting that racist Chambers. She wanted to die.

How could anyone live in this crazy patriarchy, tyrannical, racist, country?

She knew it was like this. Her family had told her, kept her safe in their bubble, so she'd be safe from the racists… The whites.

'I wanna go home,' she whispered.

She brought her hand to her face and a miracle, better than any Christmas miracle of all time: her elbow knocked on something in his inside pocket, wide and thin.

She brought her hand to her face, fingers covering her face, making a mask of fingers over her features. With her other hand she slipped the phone from Brigance's pocket, slipping it in to her pocket. She'd call the police now.

And twenty minutes later she did. And the whole mad circus came to town, came to Steel Mountain. Chambers was out of time and luck.

Chapter Nine

It was time. All this time, all the hours of planning, driving, fighting; all the pain and fear, the horror that he had done and been through.

He had taken lives on this mountain, killed fool kids who knew nothing; almost drowned in a river, lost boots, cut his feet to blood pulps; almost gone down under the heat of the sun; fought nature on this haunted evil mountain; and his journey was only half over.

He looked though the scope, readying his nerves for the kill. He was ready, his body anyway; his mind took more convincing to get under control.

The view from the scope was the same as the naked eye but sharper. He waited and wondered how much longer he should or could wait.

He moved his body twice from leaning on the tree to kneeling next to it.

His knees ached, stinging, biting pain in his kneecaps.

He would have to be careful, if he waited any longer on the cold hard rocky floor. Then his legs might go numb and that would make running almost impossible.

He shifted his body weight around, feeling the blood flow to his muscles, feeling the muscle coming back to life. He hoped he wouldn't cramp up. His back also was worrying him.

He jammed his head back to the scope.

Light, a dull, dim amber light came from the hut's doorway. His hands worked on auto-pilot

Body and mind knew some training never leaves you. It was always the same with him, he hated the wait. The cold, wet sweat coated his body. And it was nothing to do with weather. It was fear.

The cabin's door opened, Chambers watched, all of him focused on that square patch of amber light, shining on the grass.

Then a man moved in the doorway. A man's shadow fell across the woodland floor.

The man seemed giant by the look of his shadow. He moved out form the hut, looking around in the thick dark gloom of the night.

A light, bright and white, clicked on and a shaft of light shone out into the trees opposite Chambers, whose head was low next to the scope.

He closed one eye, looking though the scope. The man seemed to be alone, no one else followed him out.

So, thought Chambers, this man was about to be the first kill in the battle for the kid.

Chambers was about to commit murder. And it could all be over a corpse.

The man stood in the woods shining the light lazily around the dark, still and empty trees; he was lighting up nothing.

Their blood was up from earlier; he had seen nothing and heard nothing. Hell, that fucking fool had only just came back with the food, from Brigance's.

They were jumping at shadows. But here on this mountain, shadows were something to jump at. That knocking sound was a wild dog or something like that, that smelled the food and jumped at the wood of the hut. Hell, Cole was on edge, he was starting to frighten the others… his eyes didn't look right… almost animal. God, this place. He had been in prison many times, but here in the great outdoors… felt worse. There was something here.

No news about the money, yet.

They had to get it soon. People should fucking pay, what they owned.

That family had a fortune and yet their own kid was worth less than their fancy cars and houses.

He lowered the light, taking a pack of smokes from his blue jeans' pocket. He popped the lid, sliding one out, placing it at the side of his mouth. The smoke rested there as his fingers went to his lighter.

Chambers was about to fire using the bright white light from the flashlight to guide him, when he turned it off. Chambers' forefinger relaxed, uncurling from the trigger.

He looked on, watching, waiting. Any strange movement should be watched and understood, then when he understood he would attack.

The man went for something in his pocket. Chambers head at once brought the scope down, following the man's movement with the AK-47, ready to fire at any given time.

He lit the smoke, looking dead ahead without really looking. The only reason he had said he would do a patrol was so he could have a smoke in peace.

He had been locked in that fucking hut for days and days with the others waiting for their payday. A fucking payday that never seemed to be coming and nothing had happened, no news, no nothing.

The boy had been a pain too. Crying, begging to go home. The little piss ant! He had beaten his ass for that. The kid was a good punchbag, a good thing to ease the stress.

Soon they would put that brat in the ground, take the money and set up somewhere, anywhere, else. But far from this place.

This fucking mountain, that had been the worst. This mountain, its rocks, trees and air. There was something there, it hung in the air, entering the lungs, he thought.

He hated it here, he wished he could just go, leave, *go* form Steel Mountain. He didn't like to be in one place for too long. It made it easier for the cops to find you and that wouldn't be good. Maybe they could get off with it, if they were caught? They could play the race card.

If they got an all-white jury and the YouTube and Twitter warriors got hold of it then... maybe.

Play "the USA was born racist" card. So they had to do it because of the racism. After all, half of the world thought blacks couldn't be racist. Blacks only did what they did because of the racism in the patriarchy or whatever. But kid kidnapping was something else.

Fuck it. The cops had no money, or man power. He and the rest would be paid in a day or two. He smiled, taking a long pull on his smoke.

Chambers watched. *Just a cigarette*, he thought, as he aimed… *Wait for it*, he thought. *Wait for it… Now!*

He pulled the trigger on the AK-47.

As he pulled on his smoke a lot of things happened at once. There was a harsh, banging, crushing, smashing pain in his head, his skull. He felt as if his head was in an iron vice. His head shot backwards. The force in his head was crashing, smashing, blood oozing from his lips and noise, and from the penny sized hole in his face.

Then a great huge bang. Deafening. It echoed through the woods, moving though the great standing trees.

All in the hut heard it. At once all of them were up on their feet, looking, eyes jammed on the wooden panels and window in shock, all knowing what that sound was.

The shot man lay still, perfectly still, his cigarette in hand. He felt something else, beside the pain. He lifted his hand to his forehead, fingers touching just above his left eye, touching something wet and oozing… his own blood. He could feel the wind, blowing though his skull.

Oh God, he thought. The bullet had blown a hole right though his head. His lips opened, then shut, then reopened again and again, trying to form words. 'Shot. I'm Shot,' he tried to say as two more bullets crashed into his chest.

His body rocked back and forth then toppled over, stone cold dead.

Inside the cabin, the others stood staring, listening.

Cole, their leader, small, brutal, dark-skinned and dark-minded man, a man who was cold dark and hard, man made from ice and steel, the perfect killer.

If he had joined the army, he would be a bloody general. He was their leader in every way, and he took control of the fight that was happening.

'Get the *light*, the *light*!' Cole's powerful voice filled the room.

One of the men threw out a powerful arm which caught the small oil lamp, slapping it off the table where it smashed to the ground in a thousand pieces, and at once the hut was in darkness.

Cole looked up, seeing dark shadows everywhere.

'Stay down, stay *down*!' screamed out Cole. 'Everyone, stay down, your eyes will adjust to the dark, guns out. Stay away from the windows... for now!' he said.

Chambers, after dropping the man with the flashlight, had spun the AK towards the small and narrow windows. When the light went out, the hut had at once fallen into darkness. He couldn't see though the windows. No targets. No nothing.

Chambers made a soft pissed off clicking sound in his mouth, as he looked and waited for his targets, seeing through the scope, looking for anything, any sign that here was someone moving inside the hut. There was nothing.

Smart, these boys knew what to do, Chambers thought. He stood, moving around the tree, keeping his body low, his eyes never moving from the hut, ready to kill.

Nothing, there was no movement.

He needed a new plan. It came to his mind. His thumb went down to the selector, putting the AK-47 to full fire.

He would have to be very careful; he would fire high. He knew had to do it.

He saw in his mind's eye, the men on their hands and knees ready, waiting for something to happen, eyes on the door or windows, fingers wrapped around their weapons, hearts racing, fear in their minds; and yet a large part of them liked it. Something was happening and he would make something happen.

Chambers turned his neck and hearing a soft click, he turned his head the other way. Aiming at the cabin, he was on a ridge in the treeline looking down at the cabin. He was ready, his forefinger clicked the AK-47 into full auto. He was ready for the kill.

He fired the gun. It screamed out into the night, the front of the gun lit up with white hot fire. The gun shook, screaming. Hot empty shells flew out of the gun, smashing into the ground around him.

He fired fast and down, placing the bullets at the middle of the cabin. He had seen the kid on one side of the cabin. He wouldn't shoot there. He did move the gun to the other side, firing at the cabin's door. He kept on firing, watching great chunks of the cabin fly everywhere. All he could hear was the scream of the gun and all he could smell was the sweet, homely smell of gunpowder… This was home to Chambers. A smile broke across his face.

All the men in the hut knew the attack was coming. Chamber had guessed right. They were on the floor, bodies low to the dirt, weapons in hand, scared eyes roaming, taking quick fearful looks out of the small window. They saw nothing but the dark pines, knowing the attacker was out there hiding, waiting and watching. Weapons in hand, they knew that their friend was dead out there, they had no doubt.

The four men lay on the dirty floor, bodies pressed to the rotting wood, heads moving along looking for something, anything that could help, their guns close by, two handguns.

They had three guns: two inside the cabin, the other outside with the dead man; the man on patrol was given one of the guns.

Cole's eyes were not on the door or window. His eyes were on the shotgun, resting on the wall of the hut. They did have large Rambo style hunting knives and all of them had one of those. Strong dark fingers where constantly grasping and regrasping the knives' grips!

All three faces were worried, after hours and days of being here, in the extreme heat, dodgy water, no food for days, the kid screaming calling for his mom and dad, driving them crazy.

There were bank robberies, smash and grab raids. But kidnapping, that was something else. It was evil… they had felt it… the evil.

It was powerful, a powerful feeling, the power, the control over this kid's life, was like a drug.

They chose if he lived or died.

They all — even Cole who was the strongest mental and physically — affected by the power, they had over the kid, it was a high.

Cole looked at the kid. He was alive but only just.

Cole spoke, the first and only kind words he would ever say to the kid.

'Kid, keep your head down.'

Johnson, the man closest to Cole, hearing Cole's words, moved over to the kid, pulling him off the filthy blood and shit stained mattress. He pulled him to the ground, flipping the rusting bedframe over and in front of the kid, pushing it close to him, giving him some sort of cover.

The boy went into a ball, his thumb went into his mouth, eyes closed, heart racing though terror of what was coming.

The men could hear nothing but their own deep and sharp breaths coming in thick and fast, weapons held tight.

Johnson sat in front of the kid; knife close his chest, wondering what the hell they were going to do…

Bang. A gunshot echoed though the hut.

Splintering wood shot though the hut.

Wood dust fell gently to the ground.

Cole's eyes zoomed sharply to the panel, seeing a large and rough hole punched into and though the wall.

Then another.

Bang! It sounded more like a sledgehammer than a bullet. Before any of them could work out where that bullet hit, another bullet smashed into the hut at around shoulder height of a normal sized man. The hammering sound started again. Blows came down, hitting the walls. Hot dust fell. Wood splintered, flying around them, then great chunks of wood hit the ground, raining down like hail.

The bullets had gone straight though the wooden boards, many going straight through the hut.

Slivery moonlight shone though the holes. There was a pause that seemed like an eternity as they lay on the wooden floor.

'Keep low, he wants us to panic. So he can get clear shot at us!' whispered Cole.

Cole looked to the far end of the hut at the 12-gauge shotgun resting on the far wall. He had to go for it. He moved snake like towards it, staying out of the shifts of silver moonlight, thinking that he would somehow be seen.

He moved as fast as he dared, feeling the eyes of the others on him, as he did.

His hands grabbed, pulling the gun free from wall. In one fast move he had the shotgun in hand holding it tight.

Cole looked at the gun with pure love in his eyes. He had been weak and naked, but now with this iron and wood in his hands, he felt as if he was wearing a suit of armour. He pumped the shotgun, ready to fight back.

Cole heard it first. That's how he knew that bullet didn't kill him.

Over his head a fresh bullet hammered into the hut, just over his head. With a small cry of shock he dropped down low, even though he was on the already on the floor. He jammed his eyes shut, as hot and fast-moving wood crashed over and on to his face, making a deep red cut on it.

The next bullet hit the window a few feet away. The glass shattered, hitting the ground around them, glittering in the moonlight.

Cole looked at the glass glinting in the moonlight. He met the eyes of the others.

Cole pointed at the man with the pistol. Cole pointed at the window and the man went to it fast, staying low. Cole did the same, standing at the other side of the window. The two men stood opposite each other, at the window frame. The shooter was close.

Cole put three fingers up, then he dropped one.

Then another.

Then another.

The two men pushed their weapons out of the window, fingers pulling on the triggers of their guns. The guns lit up, screaming, as both bullets and buckshot flew out into the deep, dark woods.

The small hut came alive with red fire from the ends of the guns. The building roared with hammering explosions from the bullets.

Mouths open, teeth bared, eyes wide, the men fired at nothing and everything, until the small hut was full of a smoky, gunpowder mist.

'Stop, stop!' screamed Cole. The room was covered in the thick smoke, making it impossible to see.

Fingers fell from the triggers; smoke still went up from the ends of the guns. But quickly the smoke went out though the open window and bullet holes.

Chambers was watching the smoky building, firing random shots into it, trying to get any sign of his prey, trying to get them to show themselves.

Then the roar of bullets hammered towards him. He saw the window explode with bullets.

Bullets crashed out across the trees, into the dirt. Leaves kicked up into the air, shots smashed into the trunks of the trees. Chaos exploded around him.

Chambers watched, shocked. He was ready for a small attack, not this.

A bullet had hit a branch on the tree a few feet from where he was.

Chambers dropped down into a ball, behind the tree, the AK close to his chest, as the gunfire screamed around him.

He moved his head as bullet after bullet hit above and around him.

After what seemed an age the bullets stopped.

Chambers' ears where ringing, rage boiling in him.

He aimed the AK at the hut. He moved the gun across the building, stopping at the window.

A man moved.

Chambers' face broke into a wide evil smile. Chambers pulled the trigger.

The gun went off. A red, orange, and yellow flame erupted from the end of the rifle.

The bullet smashed though the glassless window, into the man.

The smoke rose from his pistol, he had fired. Jack, one of Cole's gang, looked out from the window of the cabin. It had been a good of idea of Cole's to do that, to flush out the rifle man.

Jack saw it, a small flash of red, orange light. Then the world went bright red, as bullet after bullet smashed down hard into his body, crashing in through and out of him, hitting all over his head, face, and neck.

The shooter lowed the gun, but still firing, Chambers' finger switched the AK-47 into fully automatic. He kept on firing at the man, now firing into the wall under the cabin's window.

Bullets smashed down on to Jack's shoulders and chest. Large sickly pieces of his flesh were ripped and thrown from the frame of his body. His flesh fell from his body, hitting the floor with sickly, wet thuds.

The other two looked on in shock as the bullets cut through him, like wet paper.

The opposite wall was covered in wet meat and holes fro, the force of the bullets.

Then just as fast as the hail of bullets had come down, it stopped. Their ears echoed from the sudden and powerful silence.

Jack still stood at the window; somehow he was still alive. Yet he was blind and deaf. Every inch of him was on fire, burning. He tried to move, his upper body twisting and twisted.

What was left of his face was trying to move, a mask of shock and pain.

Then he fell forward, his body half falling out of the hut, hanging from the window frame, his long legs and waist still in the hut.

Cole was first to get it back together. He had moved to one of the many holes in the hut's wall, and he looked out of it. He had seen the flashing red and orange from the killer's gun and knew where he was.

Chambers' finger moved off the trigger, the AK stopped screaming and shaking in his hands.

Chambers watched the man as he fell forward, jamming into the window frame.

His eyes went wide with shock at what he had just done. Then his training took over. He had seen four maybe five men. Two down.

He looked form the dead man in the window frame, to the dead man on the grass.

Chambers moved the scope, looking for movement… there was none. It was time to move.

They had an idea of where he was. It was time to go. He had to be careful, very careful. Standing, holding the

AK close to his chest, he ran into the cool shadows of the forest.

He didn't see the other man climbing over the dead one, laying on top of Jack's corpse, using at as a shield.

Chambers moved out of the shadows too soon. He stepped into a patch of silver moonlight and Cole saw him. Cole acted fast and calm.

Chambers heard it, the sound of a powerful shotgun being fired, the sound booming around him.

Buckshot slammed into a tree a few inches ahead of him. Large chunks of wood hit Chambers in the face.

Was it dust? Wood? Buckshot?

Something went right into his eyes. They burned. He dropped down. Shock and pain filled his mind.

Chambers stopped dead, fingers raking into his face, trying to get his vison back.

At the same time, a voice strong in his mind, a drill instructor it seemed was screaming out at him. To get up and to run. He did, bolting into the dark, still pretty much blind. His version was dark and red. He just about made out shapes, his eyes were burning and watering.

He made one step, two steps… *Bang!*

Something — a bullet? — hit his hip and upper thigh. Buckshot had hit Chambers' skin, ripping it open, pain flowing through his body.

He went up and over, crashing into the woodland. The AK shot out of his hands, lost to him.

His hands went to the 357 magnum. Pulling the gun out, he fired three quick shoots, then stopped.

He started firing wildly, towards the hut.

A shot from Chambers' gun had just missed Cole, the bullet crashed into the dead man, blood and meat smashing into Cole face.

Cole screamed ,jumping away, hands up as he fell down. The shotgun crashed into the ground, as a dead man's blood smashed into his eyes.

Johnson screamed and screamed, moving to a corner of the cabin as all hell seemed to be breaking lose. His screams where mixed with the little boy's.

'The world is ending. The world is ending,' Johnson said over and over, childlike, as bullets hammered everywhere.

Chapter Ten

Oh God, thought Chambers, hip burning. A flood of fiery pain was crashing through his body, yet again.

He had dropped the AK-47, it was lost in the pine.

If he was honest with himself he didn't know how many bullets he had left in his pocket for the Magnum. His hand went into his pocket, meeting nothing but air.

Hell, with the buckshot his pants could have ripped. His ammo could be laying somewhere on the floor.

Three bullets left, he thought. *Shit.* The powerful pistol would be empty soon.

He had to move. He pulled himself along, towards the woods on his hands and knees.

Blood ran down the side of his mouth and oozed from the buckshot in his leg. He spat out a mass off blood, which hit the roots of a large tree that he passed.

Chambers moved without thinking. He was in pain and wanted to keep out of the way of that powerful 12-gauge shotgun.

The shotgun blazed out across the woodland, buckshot smashing into the trees and grass. Pieces of wood and dirt went flying into the night sky.

Chambers couldn't help it. He let out a shocked cry. He pulled himself to his feet. His hip let out a scream. But he bolted as fast as he could, hands over his head, zooming away until his foot tripped over a root. He went down, his bad hip smashing powerfully down on the harsh, rocky woodland floor. An explosion of pain went through his brain from his hip.

Chambers' eyes opened wide until it looked as if his they were about to pop from his head. His mouth opened in a shocked scream but he quickly forced his jaw closed to stop the sound from giving him away.

Another blast filled the night air. Chambers took a deep breath, filling both his nose and mouth with the night air, tasting the forest air and the thick heavy blue gun smoke.

His chest was rising high, lungs burning.

Chambers' body was aching, hip screaming, head pounding, and he was alone. Lost in this thick wood. No back up. No nothing, just him. He had killed two. But he was injured and outnumbered.

Cole was laying on top of the corpse he had once viewed as a friend, now a meat sandbag.

He pumped the shotgun, thinking about the ammo had had left.

He was sure that he had hit *him*. That bastard out there in the pines. He was sure that son of bitch was hurt. But he was far away, he could have just glanced him. Hell, he could have just pretended to be hit.

No, he thought. *I know I hit him.*

With widening eyes he saw movement. Something moved, bobbing up and down and to the left.

He fired the shotgun at it, finger pulling back on the trigger, all the way back. His finger shot forward again, the other hand pumping the pump of the shotgun. He felt the warm hiss as the hot empty bullet case whizzed by his bare arm, clattering down to the floor.

Then a loud and powerful gunshot hit the bullet ridden hut.

A fresh and large bullet hole smashed into a wooden panel. It split the wood in two, cutting it open, making a huge gash. Having already been hit several time, the panel gave way, dropping to the floor with a crash. The building was starting to fail, as that one panel took out two more that fell to the ground.

Cole dumbly looked at the hut's walls as another bullet crashed into the building, this one close to the window frame.

Cole pulled himself away from the window, landing in a heap, in the corner of the room, eyes closed face away, as another bullet hit near him.

Whatever this gun was, it was powerful.

Large chunks of hard wood went flying around their bodies.

Chambers had moved to his, feet testing his hip. It burned like a son of a bitch, but he could move! Goddam it, he hurt so *bad*! But he was moving.

He made it to another tree, dropping down under its branches.

This one was closer to the hut. He had to move closer, he had little time. The pain in his leg was overpowering; soon it could make him pass out, then it was over.

Time to go in for the attack. He dropped low, looking at the hut. Hell, gun smoke was still rising from it, as if it was on fire. Hell, this was hell.

Chambers eyes raked hard on the woodland floor looking for his beloved AK-47. But even with silver white light from the moon, there was little to no visibility.

His eyes zoomed over and over, moving over the ground, seeing nothing but dark shapes in the gloom. His AK could be here. Here, there, anywhere.

Each stick or branch on the ground could be his gun or not, and his eyes were still watering from the tree dust. His vison came back a little at a time.

He let loose a soft swear word to the chilly night air.

Chambers looked at the 357 magnum.

He aimed at the side of the wooden house.

He pulled on the trigger.

The gun screamed out; his aim was off. He'd hit a random part of the hut.

Lowering the gun, he moved off, low down waiting for the return fire… nothing.

He moved snake like across the dirt, towards the hut, but still kept back from it. He aimed and fired once then twice.

He opened the gun. All bullets used. His hand went into his pocket… empty. He remembered.

His face was cold and ready. He dropped the 357, leaving it on the grass. Taking out the Beretta storm, he aimed it. He fired.

The bullets went through the wood of the building but were nowhere near as powerful. The gun rocked much more gently then the 357. Chambers carefully fired again, lowering the gun.

He waited, thinking, wanting the best shot, wondering how many were left. He had only killed two for sure; had any of the bullets he had fired since he killed the man in the window, hit anyone else? Or was it all a waste?

Cole was back at the window. He was on his knees under the window frame, gun in hand, the shotgun sticking out of the window frame.

Without looking, without aiming, he pushed the shotgun out the window frame, blasting two fast pumps with the shotgun.

Chambers hit the ground, as a mound of grass and mud blew up around him, grass and dirt hitting him the face and the rest of his body. He moved hand over hand, hip scraping on the ground, sending shock waves of pain through him.

Without thinking Chambers moved to the hut, as the mad man fired the shotgun out the window. Not aiming just firing. Chambers was close to the door... so close.

Cole stopped firing, waiting for a target, getting a grip of himself. Waiting, for what seemed like an age, waiting for the return fire to come crashing around him. But nothing happened.

He's moving, Cole thought.

The walls of the hut creaked ominously, as if there were about to fall down at any second.

He looked at Johnson hiding in the corner, a knife in hand, the kid behind him.

Cole moved back to the body at the window, still using it as cover. He moved carefully around the window, making sure that he was hard to see. He looked all around. Looking for his pistol the dead man had.

Where the hell was it? he thought.

He dropped to his knees, hands slapping down childlike on the floor trying to feel for the gun, in the dark, finding nothing. Then his dark, smart eyes looked down over the edge of the window, staying as low down as he could; just under the dead man's hand on the grass and dirt was his gun.

He jumped over and across the dead man, laying on top of his body, his fingers searching, eyes going from gun to the treeline, knowing at any second a bullet could hit him.

He had it, gun in his hand. He snatched the gun and fell back inside the falling down hut.

Cole looked at the gun in his hand, then over to Johnson. Only him and Johnson left now, and the boy. Johnson only had a knife. Should he give him the pistol and he would keep the shotgun or both for him, he thought.

Better with two of them having guns. Better chance of surviving.

'Johnson… Johnson!' Cole spoke in a whisper.

Johnson had been looking around him as if he could see their attacker though the wood of the building. He heard him, looking into Cole's cold hard eyes stabbing into his.

Cole looked to the kid, a thin helpless thing. The boy's mind was like an egg shell with a large gash across it. Soon it would break. He was just screaming, non-stop. Screaming and screaming and screaming. Odd, thought Cole, he hadn't noticed, then as a piece of the cabin fell down behind him, realised why he hadn't heard.

Johnson read the message in Cole's eyes. Johnson moved towards the kid and with two powerful blows, he slammed his fist into the kid's chest and head. The first blow smashed into his rib cage, pushing the air out of his body. The kid's body shot upright, then the next punch came in smashing into his face, cutting the skin above his right eye. A long thin red line of blood leaked from his head.

The kid's eyes rolled into his skull as he passed out. The screaming stopped. Now he couldn't shout out any help to the attacker, who must be here for the kid. And Cole wasn't about to give an inch to that bastard out there. Not one inch.

Chambers' breath came in and out, in sharp and shallow, his lungs were burning and not working fully.

The world was starting to twist and turn around him. His head was burning.

His brain was not getting enough oxygen.

His body was starting to fail. The buckshot in his hip was burning too much. His body was low on power.

He felt like a racing car losing oil that had to press on. But he wasn't a car. There was no pit team waiting for him. He was a human. And soon he would pass out, he'd get killed, or do something dumb, like get himself killed.

Chambers wished for water. He wished his head to be still and clear. He wished he wasn't here. And even more he wished he didn't have to be here. It was time.

Chapter Eleven

The hut seemed smaller than normal. Cole was still, the shock of the attack by the unknown person was starting to wear off.

He lay low with the powerful shotgun in hands.

The rate of fire then almost stopped, and the weapon had changed.

By his feet, two bullets smashed into the walls.

Both men's eyes whizzed to the back of the hut.

Chambers was ready. He lowered the Berretta Storm, seeing the smoke raise from the end.

He moved quickly and as quietly as he could, standing a few feet from the edge of the hut, gun in his hands.

He limped towards the door.

As Cole and Johnson looked at the fresh holes in the wall, their eyes and attention had turned from the door, as Chambers hoped they would.

Cole heard it first. He had time to let out a cry of shock. His eyes went very wide and wildly he went for his shotgun, pulling it up and to the side as Chambers jumped, flying shoulder first towards the old worm-eaten door.

His shoulder smashed into the door, his bodyweight smashed the door open, making the door crack.

Cole was still lifting the shotgun when Chambers smashed into the hut.

Johnson screamed in shock. He saw not a man but a monster in the shape of a man, crashing inside towards Cole, and in front of him.

Cole was shocked, but fast. His finger pulled the shotgun's trigger; the thing went off. But Cole was more shocked than he thought. He hadn't pulled the shotgun high enough.

The buckshot hit the wooden floor, missing Cole's feet by inches. He could feel the heat of the buckshot though his boots.

Chambers had gone through the door at speed, his body was out of control. He slammed into the ground, splintering the wooden boards as he hit the ground hard. The pain in his hip let out a powerful scream. But the pain was nothing more than fuel for his rage, he'd turn the pain into rage.

Chambers fingers were gripped tight on the handle of his gun. Chambers saw everything; his eyes and mind seemed to be working overtime.

A man in the corner. He couldn't see the boy.

Then his whole body and mind was transfixed on Cole and the shotgun in his hands.

It was he who had shot him.

Their eyes met; both were wearing masks of hate and rage.

Cole moved fast. Chambers moved fast... not fast enough. Chambers' gun hand was pinned at his side; he should have kept it up and ready to fight.

Cole raised his gun at Chambers.

It was over. Cole's gun was aiming right at him. He pumped it, aiming right at Chamber's face.

Cole fired.

Chambers rolled, twisting his body away, as fast he could from the shotgun, all of this in a matter of seconds. He rolled away from the gun, his knees burning, hip, on fire. He heard the shotgun speak, as he turned as fast as he could.

He felt the hot stinging buckshot fly past him, cutting his shirt on his back, tearing it open. Pieces of his shirt fell from his back, as the skin on his back opened, blood bloomed there. But he was lucky, the buckshot had only cut into his back shallowly.

Finger lines of blood bloomed over his back. He screamed, hands going for his back and the gun fell from his hands.

How did I miss him? Cole bellowed inside his mind.

Cole's hands moved to the shotgun's pump and he pumped I, aimed and fired.

Chambers rolled his body. He hit a wall, eyes raking the wood floor looking for his pistol, when another blast form the shotgun fire happened behind him.

Buckshot crashed over his head.

Johnson, in pure fear, started to fire without really aiming, the terror unloosed in his mind.

Johnson fired everywhere, anywhere, missing both Chambers and Cole by inches.

Bullets crashed around him. Chambers was still going for Cole as there was little else he could do.

Chambers was fighting, while waiting to die; soon a bullet or buckshot would hit his body and kill him.

Chambers twisted his body around, and as he did, Cole was ready with the shotgun. About to fire. Chambers' hand went down to his side, his fingers pulling the subcompact storm from his side, and without looking or aiming he pushed the gun towards Cole and fired once.

Cole's hand was pulling back on the pump when the bullet from the subcompact hit him in the chest, but at the same time a bullet crashed into Chambers.

Johnson had him in a clean shot. All Johnson had to do was fire.

He pulled back on the trigger, the gun spoke, one bullet flow out then the gun went click. With his last shot, he hit Chambers' shoulder. A wound opened. Blood sprayed out. The bullet knocked out flesh and bone.

Chambers felt the bite of the bullet, his body went tight as a drum. Chambers looked down seeing his blood, but also Cole's.

Cole gasped, as blood fell from his mouth, blood ran across and down his chest, a star like hole was forming in his chest. The shotgun slipped from his hands.

Chambers' body smashed into Cole. He grabbed the shotgun from the ground, twisting his body upwards Cole, as fast as his wounds would let him. Chambers felt weak, wet, sickly hands on his back, as Cole tried to fight; even with his injuries, he tried to fight, knowing what Chambers was trying to do.

Cole was hit in his right lung, it was bleeding into his ribcage, he couldn't get air into his body and brain fully, his reactions were gone.

Chambers had the shotgun. He had twisted his body, holding the gun one handed.

Chambers pushed the barrel of the shotgun into Cole's chest. Their eyes meet for a flash that seemed to last for hours. Chambers' face went dark; he wanted this man dead and he fired.

The shotgun shell smashed into Cole's chest high and to the left, blowing Cole's heart into a bloody, red, pulp. All of this took about five seconds.

Cole's mind went blank.

Chambers rolled away from Cole's corpse.

Pain shot though Chambers' legs, rushing into his mind. His eyes rolled into his head. He was going to pass out. The other man would kill him, then the kid. He had failed.

But somehow, even with all his injuries, he manged to stay conscious, hanging on with all his strength, all his willpower, he stayed here and awake.

But it was close. His vision went dark, then red, as his head rolled. His shock and pain pumped through his mind, his brain working overtime. His brain forced chemicals into his body, keeping him awake and alive.

Chambers' head rolled down, then he shook it, forcing himself to stay awake. He eased back on his heels and his hand dropped to the subcompact that had fallen from his hands after he had fired that one shot. He picked it up, not knowing if the shotgun had any bullets left.

Johnson watched, shocked; he had killed Cole! Terrified, he grabbed the boy from behind the rusty bedframe. One arm around the boy's chest, he looked at his gun. Empty. He dropped it, brought his knife up to the boy's neck.

One hard pull and the kid's neck opens! he thought, pressing the blade deeper into his neck, making a small but deep hole in the throat.

A line of crimson was running down the blade!

Chambers aimed at Johnson's head.

'Hey… don't do nothing stupid, man! I'm a good shot!' said Chambers.

Pain. His voice strong but sickly with pain.

'If you shoot at me, motherfucker, you better kill me! It's me or him,' Johnson said, pushing the knife in deeper.

'Take it easy, take it easy. No one else has to die!'

'What do you want!' shouted Johnson, spit falling from his lips.

'I said take it easy!' called out Chambers. His finger was aching to pull the trigger, as his head spun.

Chambers had to make a move and do it fast, he would pass out soon. His head lowered. He was fighting this man and his own body.

'You don't tell me nothing!' barked out Johnson.

'Easy. Easy,' Chambers whispered.

Chambers moved one hand away from the gun, holding it out, palm up and open. The international sign of don't do it.

'Don't hurt him. Please. Let him go and just go. I want shoot you.'

Johnson looked down at the child, looking at the small beaten boy in his hands. A knife in his neck. The handle turned towards his hand.

Fuck the kid. Fuck this guy. Fuck it all.

The kid was rich.

He had love; Johnson never had.

Things like that would always be hidden from him. *Fuck the world and everyone in it.*

Chambers looked at Johnson. Their eyes met hard. Chambers he had seen eyes like that, every time he looked in the mirror.

Chambers focused his aim.

The world span. He tried to hold on. He couldn't. He opened his mouth.

He lowered his head, throwing up all over the floor, head bent but his eyes still on Johnson, they never moved.

Chambers' eyes burned and watered, but he still had a shot.

Johnson had had it, with everything, with life; he was done, and the kid was done to. He pushed the knife, his forearm's muscle moved.

Chambers saw the muscle move and in one quick movement, his gun spoke.

Johnson's head shot back as he fell into the wall, a small hole in the top of his head.

The kid hit the ground. Chambers slid down to the floor.

So much death was around him. Darkness took Chambers, the world just went away.

Chapter Twelve

Chambers woke. He had no idea how long he had been passed out. He blinked, looking around the dim room. He rolled over; his body hurt, he was cold and numb.

Chambers dragged himself over towards the kid, seeing the outstretched dead body of Johnson.

He looked in shock at the little body of the boy, still laying on top of the dead man.

He wasn't moving. Blood was dripping from his neck, his eyes open looking up. Eyes looking without seeing. Dead eyes.

Chambers froze. No. He couldn't be dead! Not after all he been though. He had to be alive. Chambers willed it, then, *Thank God!* The boy's chest rose. *He's alive, oh my God. He's alive!* Chambers thought.

Hot tracks of tears fell his face.

The boy was alive! But his throat was cut.

Why didn't Johnson just go? He didn't have to die. And yet he was dead. And he had almost killed a little boy and for what? It was then when Chambers' mind started to come undone.

He wanted to push away his hate, but couldn't. Years of anger, years of rage, years of resentment burst in his mind.

He did hate them... Niggers had ruined his life! Yes, he had killed that black, but... he was told to. He was the wrong man, but he didn't know. The cops fucked it up, not him. Why was he the world's punching bag?

He thought that he was helping the world. One less killer. But he didn't know it was the wrong man. Why? Why had it happened to him?

His life fell apart in a flash. The shouts, the screams. Drummed out of the force. A job he loved, a job he was good at.

The army was closed to him. The look on his father's face. He turned his back on him. Everyone had turned on him. The Nazis, the hate filled had wanted him. But he didn't want them.

The woke people were just as bad the people the people they claimed to hate.

He was lost. Alone. Wanted by no one. Lost in the pine woods. He had to do this. Hunt people for money.

He hated them all: Blacks, Whites, Asians, all of them, all people and all things were his enemy.

Chambers looked down.

This case had been the worst. He had killed four blacks, and the others, at least six dead. He had shot them down, all of them. Hell *they,* the police, the world, would blame him for all of this nightmare. Hanna would drop him in it.

He was alone.

They would say he did it all, taking the boy. He would burn. And Hanna would pull the switch.

I should kill the boy! he thought.

He lowered his gun to the kid's small, blood-stained head.

One quick pull on the trigger then the boy's pain would be gone. Then the same for him?

His Beretta pointed it down at the child's head. Then he saw him: a boy, a kid, a child. Taken, broken, beaten, cut. His hands were bright red, the skin cut so deep. Blood oozed from the wounds. The kid made a small cry of fear and pain. It was the saddest thing Chambers had ever seen.

He didn't see a black boy or his opportunity to use the boy to get freedom or money. He saw a young child, lost and scared, beyond anything that anyone should have to go though.

Fresh tears rolled down Chambers' face. He cried in shock and hate at himself.

He wasn't a racist, he was just angry at the hand the world had given him. He dropped to his knees. The gun fell. He placed his hands gently on the kid's hand, whispering softly in his ear, 'You're safe, you're safe.' He cut the ropes with a piece of glass. He pulled of his shirt, tearing it in to straps, gently tying them around his wrists. Using them as a badge. He rubbed the blood from the kid's face.

He lifted him, holding him in his arms, the kid's face close to his chest.

Chambers walked to the door stepping out into onto Steel Mountain. He limped out into the dawn light, his shoulder burning.

He had a long way to go with the kid in his arms.

He hoped he could walk, with his bad hip.

He wondered if they could get over the river.

He prayed the bike was still there.

He wished he could get the boy of the mountain safely.

He hoped Hanna would forgive him.

He hoped at long, long last he would be seen as a man, and not a racist, white man…

He hoped, as he held the boy close. He walked away from the hell that was behind him.

He hoped his body could take the hike. He had buckshot in the hip, and a bullet in his shoulder.

As the light of the sun hit them, the boy blinked, opening his eyes and looking around.

He looked up into Chambers' face and knew he was safe. He had never seen him before and yet he knew he was safe. At last, he was safe. He looked at the man's face not seeing his race or gender.

'Thank you,' the kid whispered hoarsely.

Chambers cried. In the silence. Chambers smiled softly as the fresh warm golden light as hit his face. Chamber was… free. No, they were *both* free.

"I know who I am."

"No, you don't." whispers a voice from the shadows.